FRENCH KISS

THE SILVER COVE SERIES

JILL SANDERS

GRAYTON

SUMMARY

For the next few weeks, all Lilith has to do is run the prestigious East Haven Resort while her best friend Sarah is on her honeymoon. No big deal, except it, means she'll be dealing directly with the head chef, Adam, who is not only cocky, arrogant, and French, but damn sexy to boot. This was going to be the longest two weeks of her life.

Adam really enjoys seeing Lilith riled up and flustered. Actually, it's what gets him out of bed every morning. But when someone else is threatening to sweep in and take her away, he realizes it's time to stop playing games and go after what he wants.

*L*ilith stood on the large boulder, occasionally glancing out at the vast open space behind her. When she saw her best friend, Sarah, walking towards them in a white flowing dress, she didn't think there could be a more perfect day than today. The off-the-shoulder vintage dress was perfect for Sarah's wedding. And the ring of flowers her mother had made for her hair really accented the natural feel of their wedding.

There were over three dozen guests standing on the large boulder face at the top of the hill. As Sarah walked towards them, soft music played from two speakers set up near the back.

Lilith smiled at the way Ben watched his bride walk towards him. He looked so handsome in his tan cotton suit with his hiking boots. His best man, Rowan, stood off to the side, looking just as dashing.

Lilith, for her part, was dressed in a soft pink version of Sarah's dress, but a tad shorter. Underneath both of their dresses were matching hiking boots, so they could easily climb the hill to the wedding spot.

As the preacher started talking, Lilith's eyes roamed over the crowd. She didn't know Ben's family, but his parents didn't look too thrilled to be hosting the wedding in the wide open. Ben's sister, Bella, looked beyond thrilled. Actually, she looked the happiest out of all the guests. She too had flowers in her hair, which Lilith and Crystal had arranged.

Then her eyes landed on Adam Carriveau and her heart skipped a beat. Her eyes narrowed as she took in everything about him. The man had been put on earth just to torture her.

Quickly, before he could notice her looking at him, she turned her head away. The rest of the ceremony, she tried not to feel his eyes on her, but she knew that he was watching. Her body heated up under his gaze.

When Sarah and Ben finally kissed, the small crowd erupted into loud cheers. Lilith took Rowan's arm and walked back down the hillside with him, chatting about his latest job. The man was a doctor. And a damn sexy one at that.

Why did she feel so comfortable around him, but felt like her entire body was on fire around Adam? Both men were tall, sexy, blue-eyed, and were in professional careers. Maybe it was because Adam did everything he could to just plain irritate her.

Since his first day working at East Haven Resort, Adam had said and done things to get in her way.

If customers asked for substitutions on food items, he'd treat her like it was her idea. Every time he talked to her, he'd lay on the thick French accent, even though she'd overheard him talking to Sarah or one of the other staff members without it.

Once, she'd walked in to the kitchen as he was talking with one of the waiters, and he'd been telling the guy that any woman he dated had better conform to his wishes and do everything in her power to please him. She'd gotten so pissed, she'd actually dropped a glass, causing the pair to realize that she was eavesdropping on them. Instead of getting embarrassed, he'd just smiled at her like he'd known she was there all along.

Then there was the time he'd kissed her… She started to close her eyes, but then remembered they weren't all the way down the hill yet. She stumbled slightly, but Rowan's arm rushed around her and steadied her.

"Thanks," she mumbled.

"It's probably hard to hike in a long dress," he said, shifting her weight so that he took most of it.

"No, not really. I guess I was just lost in thought," she admitted.

"About?" His blue eyes bore into hers.

She was not going to open up to Rowan about Adam, so she lied. "I'm going to miss Sarah. I know they're only going to be gone on their honeymoon for a few weeks, but…" She let the rest drop.

"From what I hear, you're more than capable of handling things at the resort."

"Sure I am." She smiled, remembering how Sarah had given her a raise and the title of co-general manager. "I meant on a personal level." She sighed. "I feel like things are going to change now," she said, sidestepping a puddle of water.

"She's still going to be the same old Serenity," Rowan

added, causing Lilith to giggle. "What?" He helped her the rest of the way down the path.

"It's still so funny to hear her called that." She shook her head.

"Only family calls her that," Rowan said, stopping at the mouth of the trail as the other guests walked by them.

"Yes, I know, but..." She stopped when someone bumped into her from behind.

"Sorry." The French accent was thick this time. "I don't think we've met." Adam held out his hand to Rowan. "I'm Adam Carriveau."

"Rowan Holley, I'm Ser... Sarah's cousin," he corrected as he shook Adam's hand.

"Oh, oui. I've heard so much about you."

"As have I about you. I haven't made it out to the resort to enjoy one of your meals yet."

"No need to, I was put in charge of the dinner tonight." His eyes moved to Lilith's and she felt her spine straighten. "You are coming, oui?" His blue eyes bore into her own.

"Yes," Rowan answered, causing Adam to glance over at the forgotten man.

"Bien, I will see you there." Adam's eyes moved once more to Lilith's. "Lilly," he whispered, then turned and walked away.

"What was that all about?" Rowan leaned closer and whispered next to her ear.

She shivered slightly, knowing it had nothing to do with Rowan's breath on her face. "He's conceited," she answered, a little too loudly. She heard Adam chuckle as he walked away and felt her face heat.

She was determined to have a good time for her friend,

but it was going to be next to impossible if Adam was going to be underfoot for the rest of the night.

"Well, shall we?" Rowan held out his arm, waiting for her to take it.

Just then, Adam glanced back towards them as he stopped in front of his car. Pasting on a smile, she took Rowan's arm and followed him to his car. She'd ridden to the wedding with Sarah and her mother, but she figured riding with Rowan to the reception would be just the trick she needed to prove to Adam that the kiss between them had meant nothing.

CHAPTER 1

*A*dam tried to keep calm, but the woman was driving him nuts. Okay, maybe it wasn't all her fault. After all, he'd spent almost six months skirting around showing her exactly what he felt for her. But, in all truth, he doubted he could be more obvious.

In all his twenty-five years, he'd never had to work so hard to win a woman before. He was pretty sure everyone knew exactly how he felt about the sexy woman except the woman herself. What he wouldn't give to run his fingers through those thick sandy-blonde tresses with those mesmerizing auburn highlights streaking through them. Sure, there had been the heated kiss in the kitchen one night, but Ben had walked in less than a minute after he'd laid his lips over those sexy plump ones of hers, and he hadn't gotten the taste he'd craved. Or been able to show her exactly how he felt about her.

Now he watched another man zero in on the woman he was pretty sure had stolen his heart. He felt his blood begin to boil, so he turned back to finishing the final touches for the wedding dinner.

He'd worked long and hard for this night. Sarah's wedding to Ben was the perfect setting to prove he was the right man for the job.

Actually, he rather liked catering weddings and at one point had dreamed about opening his own wedding catering business.

He'd been grateful that he had been given free rein on the menu. Sarah and Ben had left everything in his capable hands, including the design of the wedding cake.

It had taken him less than ten minutes to finalize the full menu for the small event. He had started out with two hors-d'oeuvres, the sweet Maryland crab cakes with herb rémoulade and his personal favorite, smoked salmon on lemon herb blini with dill crème fraiche and caviar. He'd followed them up with his butternut squash soup with ginger which, from the looks of the empty bowls returning to the kitchen, had been a big hit. The salad had been tougher to choose, but he'd chosen the crab and lobster Louie with horseradish panna cotta topped with avocados over a simple autumn salad with fruit.

There was just something about adding crab and lobster to greens that he found pleasing.

For the main course, he'd let Sarah and Ben choose from a list of choices. They had both agreed on the roasted filet mignon with potato leek galette, sautéed spinach, and roasted vegetables for one main dish, with his specialty, almond crusted salmon with aged red wine sauce, as the other.

Everything was perfect, except for the fact that he

couldn't keep his mind off the image of Lilith sitting next to another man in the next room as he slaved over a hot stove.

He'd had a hard time taking his eyes off her during the ceremony in the soft pink flowing dress that clung to her tan shoulders. Her sexy auburn hair was tied in a loose braid that flowed down her back and had small flowers tucked in each fold. She'd been simply breathtaking.

"Go," he heard behind him and turned to see Rob, his sous chef, glaring at him. "We've got this. Go, your mind isn't in here anyway." Rob turned back to his task at hand. Then a hand reached in and took the pan of onions, which had clearly been overcooked, from the fire. He frowned as he watched Tara walk to the sink and dump them in. She glanced over her shoulder and nodded.

"Go, your time is better spent out there anyway."

He sighed and watched her wipe out the hot pan, no doubt getting it ready to redo what he'd screwed up.

He'd hired some of the best staff around for the resort, and he'd brought them along for the night as well. Even though the resort kitchen was sitting empty for the night, he knew they were right. His mind was elsewhere, and he wasn't benefiting his staff by being in the way.

Wiping his hands, he straightened his jacket and took a cleansing breath before stepping out of the small kitchen at Sarah's family home. He'd been impressed at the size of the place, even though he'd have preferred cooking for the intimate event back in East Haven Resort's bigger kitchen. Still, here the kitchen noises were easily drowned out by the laughter and sounds of the party from the next room.

When he stepped through the swinging doors of the

kitchen, his eyes moved around the room, which was packed tight with more than three dozen guests. He zeroed in instantly on the auburn-haired beauty sitting next to the blond man. Rowan's arm was resting behind Lilith's shoulders in a very casual but intimate manner.

Stepping forward, he gained the attention of a few of the guests, including Rowan.

When Lilith noticed that the man was no longer looking in her direction, her hazel eyes moved slowly towards him.

He hadn't realized the room had grown quiet until he heard clapping.

"Adam, you've outdone yourself." Sarah stood and moved towards him. "It still amazes me that I was lucky enough to snatch you up for East Haven." She walked over and wrapped her arms around him, then leaned back. "We've talked about little else except how wonderful everything is."

His smile was quick. "You do know how to stroke a man's ego." He laid on the accent heavy as he rubbed his hand over her shoulder. "You make the most lovely bride." What was the use of being a Frenchman if you didn't flatter every woman in the room? He watched her cheeks flush as her husband walked over and wrapped an arm around her shoulders. Seeing the two of them together caused a slight longing to grow in his heart, so he looked away and focused his eyes on Lilith, who quickly looked down at her nearly empty plate.

"Come, join us. Surely, you're done in the kitchen by now," Ben said, motioning towards an empty chair on the opposite side of Lilith. "We have room. Carmen and Troy had to leave early."

He nodded slightly, then took the empty spot. "How has everyone enjoyed their meal?" he asked when he sat down.

For the next few minutes, he listened to everyone compliment him. Everyone, that is, except Lilith.

How could one man be so irritating? Lilith sat across the table from Adam and listened to him talk about his favorite subject. Himself. Sure, he spent a few minutes complimenting Brittany, one of Sarah's mother's yoga instructors. The woman had annoyed her throughout the entire dinner; she had spent so much time flirting with every man at the table that it was obvious the only reason she was there was to hook up. And from the looks of it, Adam was a willing participant.

At least Rowan wasn't paying the busty brunette much attention. Instead, he leaned closer to her and asked her questions about her work and family. The former she quickly answered, the others she avoided easily enough.

She asked him how he'd chosen the medical profession and listened to him briefly talk about his time away at school. From what she'd learned about him from Sarah, Rowan was a hard worker, determined to help others, and had always put the needs of his family and friends before his own.

So, why was she finding it hard to focus on what he was saying and was instead eavesdropping on Adam's conversation with Brittany?

Just then, Ben stood up and tapped his fork on the crystal champagne glass. Hers was still half filled with the blush champagne she'd almost forgotten. Reaching over, she took the glass and downed the rest of the sweet liquid. She made the mistake of glancing towards Adam and almost choked on the swallow when his blue eyes met hers and his smile grew.

"We'd like to thank everyone for coming today to help us celebrate this special day," Ben said, breaking into her thoughts. Her eyes moved to the end of the table and she couldn't stop her smile from growing as she saw the pure happiness in her friend's eyes. Sarah's eyes and face glowed with love as she watched Ben talk to their guests. "I know this is normally the job of the best man." Everyone quickly glanced at Rowan, sitting beside her. Rowan smiled and nodded, then waved his hand towards Ben. "But, with his permission, I've asked to make the toast instead." He held up his champagne glass and waited for everyone else to do the same. She reached for hers, only to find it empty.

Adam snapped his fingers and two waiters rushed forward to fill any empty glasses, including hers.

Ben waited then cleared his throat and looked down at Sarah.

"Words can't even begin to express how much I fell for you. I could never have dreamed of meeting someone as wonderful as you. My entire life has seemed like a dream since the first moment you fell into my life."

"From what we've heard, you were the one doing the falling," one of Ben's friends added, causing the entire room to erupt in chuckles.

"Fair enough." Ben smiled, then reached down and pulled Sarah up to stand next to him. When his free arm wrapped around her waist, everyone quieted once more. "I took one look at you and lost myself. Now that you're a part of me, I feel whole again. I love you so much, Sarah." He leaned down and placed a soft kiss on her lips, then leaned back to wipe a tear gently from her cheek. "To Mrs. Rothschild." He raised his glass as she raised hers.

"To Mr. and Mrs. Rothschild," Rowan called out, earning more cheers.

Two hours later, Lilith watched her best friend, the only one she'd ever had, rush towards the car she'd helped decorate in tissue paper, old soda cans, and shoe polish. Tears streamed from her eyes as they disappeared down the street.

When an arm wrapped around her waist, she didn't tense but, instead, leaned back against Rowan and sighed. "I'm going to miss her."

"It's only two weeks," he added, chuckling.

"Two weeks and she'll be starting her new life." She sighed again before pulling away. When she turned, she smiled and realized she'd probably had a little too much pink champagne.

"I'd better go help Crystal clean up." She started to turn away.

"Leave it, my mother and aunt can handle it. Besides, they have help tonight." He nodded towards Adam, who was busy coordinating the cleanup with several of the staff from East Haven.

Instantly, she felt bad. She was staff, too. Which meant she should be there, clearing the tables and helping.

"Take a walk with me?" Rowan asked, holding out his arm for her to take.

"I should really…" she started to say, biting her bottom lip.

"Take the evening off and walk? Besides, what are you going to do? Ruin your bridesmaid dress doing dishes?" He smiled. "Relax. Serenity didn't want you lifting a finger tonight. Her words, not mine." He lifted his hand as a pledge.

She released a deep breath. "Okay, I guess I could use some fresh air to let some of this champagne settle." She wrapped her arm in his and strolled to the end of the driveway.

She felt a shiver on the back of her neck and glanced back just in time to see Adam turn away and walk back into the house.

"I always loved living here," Rowan said as they walked down the empty street. Most of the guests had followed Sarah and Ben and had quickly left, which left the streets empty and dark.

"I would have loved having a family like yours and Sarah's." She glanced over to see the bright lights from Sarah's mother's house. She knew the house which sat across from it was Rowan's. It too was brightly lit up at the moment.

"It must have been wonderful growing up so close to family."

"It had its moments." He stopped and turned towards her. "You never answered my question."

She waited and raised her eyebrows in question.

"Where did you grow up? I hear a little bit of south in your voice."

She nodded, feeling the lump in her throat tighten. "Mississippi," she answered quickly.

"I've never been." He turned and started walking again. "Do you have family there still?"

She shrugged. "Some." She followed him towards a bench near the edge of his side yard. When she sat next to him, he leaned back and put his arm behind her shoulders. He'd sat like that for most of the evening. She supposed he was trying to gauge how she would react. Either that, or he was trying to make a statement that he was interested. Either way, she felt comfortable leaning back against his strong arm.

"Any brothers or sisters?" He continued his questioning.

She shook her head, wishing she could think of another topic.

"I always wished I had a brother," Rowan said.

Lilith turned slightly. "You had Sarah."

"Having a cousin as a sister doesn't replace the desire to have a brother to play ball with."

She smiled. "I'm sure Sarah would have—"

His chuckle stopped her. "Yes, she was a tomboy up until a few years ago. Actually, she's one of the reasons I wanted a brother so bad."

"Oh?" She leaned back again.

"I could never win against her. If I had had a brother… maybe the two of us could have beat her in something."

She chuckled. "She's come a long way." She glanced down the dark street and worried that her friend wouldn't have as much time for her anymore. Sarah had been the one person to snap her out of her past. Her mind wandered to how much she'd needed her friend when she'd first moved to Silver Cove. Sarah had been the one to get her the job at East Haven. The one who had saved her. The only one she trusted with the truth. "So much has changed, so much is about to change."

"Still, she'll always be the same ol' Serenity."

She smiled. "You know; she hates that name."

He chuckled. "Why do you think I use it?"

She slapped at him playfully. "You love her."

"Of course, I do." He tilted his head and the streetlight played off the blond curly hair. "She's pure." His smile faded slightly as his eyes moved to the big house. "Not too many people are like that anymore."

"No." Her eyes followed his. She could see shadows moving around in the house and felt guilty once more for not helping with the cleanup. "I really should…" She started to get up.

"Are you seeing anyone?" His question stopped her. She glanced down at him, unsure how to answer. "I only ask… well, I have this thing. For my work. It's in a few weeks and… I've really enjoyed your company tonight."

She smiled and nodded. "Me too."

"Would you go with me? It's kind of formal and…"

"I'd love to. Let me know what day and I'll make sure I have the night off."

His smile grew. "I'll walk you back."

His arm wrapped around her waist again as they walked. When they reached the house, the front door slammed open and Adam rushed out. "We could use some extra help in here," he blurted out.

Rowan started to walk up the stairs, but Adam stopped him. "No, we have this." She noticed that his accent had retreated slightly.

"It's no problem at all…"

Just then his aunt stepped outside. "There you are, Rowan. The car never came to take the Willamses to the airport. Would you mind driving them? They're going to be late if they wait any longer."

Lilith felt relief flood her. The last thing she wanted to do was spend the next hour watching Adam and Rowan go toe-to-toe with one another.

"Sure." He frowned. "I'll be right there." He turned to her when his aunt disappeared back into the house. "I'll see you…" His eyes moved over her shoulder and she realized Adam was still standing there, waiting for her. "Later," he said quickly, then frowned at Adam. "Night."

"Au revoir," Adam said, curling his lips up, which looked more like he was showing off his teeth than smiling.

"What do you need from me?" she said when they were the only ones left on the porch.

"Help loading my car." He frowned down at her dress. "Did you bring a change of clothes?"

"Of course." She sighed and started to reach for the door, only to have him yank it open for her. "Fine. Change first, then meet me in the kitchen." He waited for her to walk through before disappearing towards the back of the house.

Lilith climbed the massive cherry staircase and headed to the third floor of the old colonial home Sarah had grown up in. She'd loved listening to stories of how her great-great-grandfather had built it for the woman he'd loved.

Lilith had spent her first year in Silver Cove living with Sarah on the third floor of the massive place. Even now, the place felt like home to her, more so than any other she'd had before.

She remembered seeing Rowan around all the time, but when she moved in, she saw less and less of him. She knew he'd been going through a hard time. She'd gotten into town a few months after his girlfriend, Lori Thomas had died. No one in the family, or the town for that matter, had wanted to talk about it, so she hadn't pried. She wasn't sure if they would keep her around if she went poking her nose into their private business.

When she reached Sarah's old room, she felt like crying when she saw how empty it was. She'd helped Sarah and Ben move all her stuff out weeks ago. They had bought a gorgeous place a few blocks away, a two-story Victorian home.

Lilith had always dreamed of living in a place half as nice as what Ben and Sarah had purchased. Maybe some-day, she said to herself as she changed into her jeans and sweatshirt.

Her mind drifted off to the image of herself walking through large double doors, past an entry hall full of expensive furniture, kicking off her shoes as she relaxed back on a massive sofa.

She sighed as she closed her eyes and imagined a glass of wine, the crackle and warmth of a fireplace as snow drifted down outside the large picture windows.

"You're taking too long."

Hearing Adam's voice behind her caused her to jump. Spinning around, her hand still over her heart, she glared at him.

"If you're in such a hurry..." She hadn't expected to see worry in his eyes. Anger, yes, but worry, no. "What's wrong?" She took a step closer.

"There was a break-in." He frowned down at her.

"Where?" she gasped. "East Haven?" He nodded, and she felt her head spin. "The supply shed again?"

He shook his head. "No, the kitchens. The wine cellar to be exact. I'm heading there now."

"I'll go with you." She gathered her overnight bags. She'd planned on spending the night here, in Sarah's old room, then returning to the resort first thing in the morning. But now, she wanted to get back and check on everything. After all, she hadn't even been in charge of the resort for a full hour.

"Oui." He nodded and reached to take the bag from her hands. "Is this all?"

She nodded and slid on her jacket.

"What about cleaning…"

"I left Rob in charge to finish up." He held the door open for her.

He followed her downstairs in silence. When she slid into his front seat, she closed her eyes and thought about calling Sarah to let her know. She had been twirling her cell phone between her hands and when Adam slid in next to her, he broke into her thoughts.

"Don't," he said after getting behind the wheel. "They don't need to worry. We've got this."

She turned to glare at him. "She has the right to know."

"And she will. After she enjoys her honeymoon. Would you want to worry the entire time you were in Maui?"

She closed her eyes and took a deep breath. "No."

"Bien." He backed out of the driveway and turned down the road, heading towards the dock to the private island.

"Why do you do that?" She turned slightly towards him.

"Quelle?"

She chuckled when he answered in French. "Lay it on thick?"

"I don't know what you mean." His eyes remained glued to the dark road.

"Your accent gets deeper around women." Her eyes narrowed as she looked at him. "Just who are you trying to impress?" She thought about it for a moment. "Brittany sure seemed smitten with it."

"Qui?" She was silent, so he answered in English. "Who?"

"J'ai compris," she said, I understood you, in perfect French.

"You know French?" he asked in his native tongue.

"Some." She turned to look out the window and watched the darkness pass by quickly.

"Why have you not said so before?"

"You never asked." She wanted to cross her arms over her chest but stopped herself. She knew the move showed that she was uncomfortable, and she didn't want to look vulnerable in front of him.

"There is a lot I would like to ask," he said as he pulled into the dock area. Jerry, the ferry driver, was already waiting for them.

"Evening," he said as Adam pulled onto the dock. "Heard about the trouble and thought you two wouldn't be long."

Adam sighed. "Anyone come and go lately?"

Jerry shook his head. "Just your crew for the big party," he said, locking the gate behind them.

Lilith got out of the car and followed the men to the top of the ferry, where they continued to talk about the break-in as if she wasn't there. Adam asked him questions she hadn't even thought to ask.

She leaned back against the railing and watched the moonlight flicker on the water as the boat made its way across the channel towards the private island that hosted East Haven Resort, the only other place she'd ever deemed her home.

CHAPTER 2

There was little that truly pissed Adam off. Reckless destruction was one of them. He felt his blood boil when he saw all the broken glass and the spilled wine on the floor of the big cellar.

"It's not that bad," Lilith said beside him. He turned on her.

"Not that bad?" He almost shouted it. "Half a dozen bottles of Château Lafite Rothschild, Pauillac along with several bottles of Dom Perignon are gone."

She shrugged. "Is that bad?"

"Is that…" He broke off and took a moment to steady himself. After a few cleansing breaths, he nodded. "Oui, très." He glanced around and took stock. "Plus, it appears more are missing." He stepped over the broken glass and the red liquid staining the cement floor. Counting, he felt himself grow even angrier. All in all, there were over a dozen bottles missing.

He turned back towards the two police officers standing just outside the cellar. One was around his age

23

with sandy blond hair, steel-blue eyes, and a strange grin on his face, as if he were in on a private joke. The other was a few years older, stockier, with thick dark hair and a mustache that most men would envy. He'd seen both men around town before.

"More than fifty thousand in damages," he supplied. He watched Lilith sway and reached for her. "Easy," he said under his breath. "Maybe you should go sit down."

"No." She jerked her arm away. "Fifty…" She shook her head as her eyes roamed over the wet floor. "Who? How?" She closed her eyes.

"Lilith…" The younger officer whom she'd met several times on the mainland cut into her thoughts. She remembered his name was Carl at the last second.

"Yes, Carl." She turned her back on Adam and gave the man her entire attention.

"You said there are only five people with keys to the cellar?" He moved closer to her.

"Yes…" She gulped.

"Oui," Adam stepped in, but she quickly put her hand on his arm to stop him.

"Sarah left me in charge," she said in a low tone.

"Oui, but this is my—"

"I'm in charge," she growled out. "Why don't you compile a list of what is broken or missing for these gentlemen?" She turned her back to him.

"That would be helpful," the other officer said, his eyes going over the floor. She didn't know his name and couldn't remember seeing him before. "I'm not sure what we can do if someone has already drunk…"

"No," he interrupted. "The bottles taken are more valuable. Someone knew what they were doing. Most likely they will be trying to sell them, not drink them." He glared at the man. "I will keep my eye..."

"You should leave this to the professionals," the younger officer added.

"Can you tell the difference between a bottle of Armand De Brignac Brut Gold Champagne and a bottle of Sutter Home?" he chided.

The man looked at him like he was speaking a foreign language, then nodded slowly. "Fair enough but contact us if you find anything." He pulled a card out of his pocket and handed it to Adam, who pocketed it, then turned to his task of making a list as Lilith walked out of the small room followed by the two officers.

Over the next half an hour, he touched every bottle at least once, rotating them and making sure his list was as accurate as possible. He was thankful one of the first things he'd done when hired was to spend a few days taking inventory.

"Well?" He hadn't heard Lilith and stopped himself from jumping. He turned towards the door to see her standing just outside the thick glass door.

"If my tally is correct, we are out more than fifty thousand. It appears whoever did this couldn't carry as much as they had hoped." He nodded to the now clean floor.

She closed her eyes and leaned against the doorway. "Who else has access to the keys?" she said once her eyes opened again.

"Besides you, Sarah, and myself?" She nodded. "Rob, Tara..." He thought about it. "There is an extra key locked in my drawer. When I let Joseph go last week, I took his key."

"Joseph?" She stood up. "He was the only one unaccounted for tonight."

"It's in my desk drawer," he said, then walked past her, making sure to lock the thick door behind him. He'd spent some time cleaning up the mess, so everything was back in place.

"Could he have made a copy?" she asked behind him.

He glanced over his shoulder. "No, it's marked…" He pulled out his key and frowned at the "Do not duplicate" printed into his own key.

"That doesn't stop a lot of places from making a copy." She followed him into his office.

The key was where he'd left it, locked in his top drawer in the small office behind the kitchen.

"No, no one in town—"

"I've made a copy of several keys in town like that one."

His eyes narrowed. "Where?"

"At Adler's."

"The hardware store?" She nodded.

He sat down and opened the bottom drawer, then pulled out the file on Joseph. When he found what he was looking for, he leaned back and closed his eyes and silently cursed.

"What?" she asked, walking over to lean on the edge of his desk.

"I said…" His eyes opened, and he realized what he had actually said and shook his head. "Nothing." He tossed the file down and nodded. "Joseph worked at Adler's before coming to us."

She glanced down at the paper. "I'll call…" She started to get up, but he stopped her by putting a hand on her leg.

"No, I'll do it." He reached into his pocket with his other hand, not wanting to move the other from her knee, especially since she hadn't shoved it away.

He punched the keys on his office phone and waited, his hand still resting lightly on her knee. He wondered how long she would let it rest there.

When he started talking, she stood up and walked to the other side of his small office while he relayed the information to the officer.

"Well?" she asked after he'd hung up.

"They are going to swing by and check up on Joseph."

"Wasn't he the one with his own boat?"

He nodded. "One of the officers went to school with him and remembered going fishing with him. That's one of the reasons I hired him. He wouldn't have to bother Jerry too much."

She walked over and sat in the chair across from his desk. "What now?"

"We wait." He opened his bottom drawer and pulled out his own bottle of wine, then held up a plastic glass for her. When she nodded, he poured them both a glass.

"Do you think he'll still have the wine?" she asked in between sips.

"I don't see why not."

"Where does one go to sell expensive wine?"

"The internet," he answered quickly. "Most wine buyers don't check the serial numbers on the bottles."

"Seriously?" She sat up a little. "They have serial numbers?"

He nodded. "When each bottle is worth several grand…" He stopped when she almost choked on the sip of wine. He moved over quickly and took her glass from her and forced her to stand up until she had her breathing back under control.

"Sorry," she mumbled as she shook her head. "I just assumed…"

"What?" He waited, then handed her the glass so she could take another drink of her wine.

"That he'd stolen a lot of bottles instead of—"

"Ten bottles are missing, four were broken," he supplied. She remained silent, so he leaned back against the desk and watched her sit back down.

"Did you enjoy yourself?" he asked after she took the last drink of her wine.

"Hmm?" She leaned back in the chair and watched him as he poured her more wine.

"Tonight? With Rowan?" He poured himself another glass and then took a sip himself, wanting to remove the distaste he got from just saying the other man's name.

Her lips curved up slightly. "He's an old friend." His eyebrows rose. Then her smile fell away. "Why do you care?" Her lips dipped down into a slight frown.

"I think he's not good." He hated when his anger took over; his mouth didn't seem to work under his control.

"You think…" She leaned forward and took another sip of her wine. "I think it's none of your business who I choose to spend my time with." She set her glass down. "So, why do you care anyway?" she asked again.

Instead of answering, he set his glass down next to hers and looked down at her. He was trying desperately to figure out his next move.

Before he could think through it, he took the plunge he hadn't planned on ever taking with a woman and told her the truth.

"I'm interested in you. In seeing you. Being with you." His hands took her shoulders and pulled her up until her body hit his.

When her hands rushed between them, he waited, and then quickly dipped his head until his mouth covered hers.

This kiss was nothing like the first one. Before it had been full of anger and she was pretty sure he'd just done it to shut her up, as he'd told Ben when the man had interrupted them.

No, this time, there was only desire. Pure. Complete. She felt her shoulders relax under his hands as his mouth tilted over hers. His lips parted and waited. She couldn't stop her tongue from darting out and licking his lower lip. He tasted like sweet wine, which only sent shivers shooting down towards her toes.

She'd never realized he was so much taller than her own five-eleven. His shoulders were so much wider than hers, and she moaned with delight when she felt his chest muscles jump under her fingertips.

His hips seemed to spread and engulf hers as he pushed himself against her softness. When she felt his hardness against her hips, she froze and pushed him away.

Her mouth opened and closed several times as she searched her mind for words. She must have stood there in shock for moments before she realized he was no longer paying attention to her. Instead, he'd reached over and answered the phone on his desk. She hadn't even heard it ring, due to the buzzing in her own ears.

Turning away from him, she walked towards the door

of his small office and took a few deep gulps of fresh air from the large kitchen area. She took a few more steps and leaned against the cold metal table.

"They caught him just outside of town. He had them stashed in the trunk of his car. Told them he was heading into the city to spend time with his girlfriend." His laugh caught her by surprise and she turned around to see his blue eyes sparkle.

"What?" She blinked a few times, completely shocked at the transformation of his face when he smiled.

"We make a pretty good detective duo." He stopped directly in front of her. Her eyes glanced down at his lips as he continued to smile at her.

She couldn't stop her own smile from forming. "Like Cagney and Lacey."

"I was thinking more like Sherlock Homes and Dr. Watson," he teased.

"Scarecrow and Mrs. King." She arched her eyebrows as she leaned back on the table. Her heart jumped quickly in her chest.

"Maxwell Smart and Agent 86." He nodded his head towards her.

"Mulder and Scully," she replied and watched him think for a moment.

"Inspector Clouseau and Gilbert Ponton."

"Booth and Bones," she retorted.

"John Steed and Cathy Gale. *The Avengers*," he added when she tilted her head. She remembered the remake a few years back with Uma Thurman and nodded.

"Maddie Hayes and David Addison." He shook his head in question. "*Moonlighting*," she added and watched him concede.

"My mother liked that show," he added, causing her to smile. "Bond and Moneypenny."

"Castle and Kate Beckett," she supplied quickly, balling her hands behind her. How could she have known that she'd get so turned on by a man who knew so many of her favorite shows?

"The Doctor and…" She waited, holding her breath. "Sarah Jane." She laughed.

"Good call… Sam and Dean."

"Okay." His smile grew as his blue eyes danced over her. "You got me on that one. I love those guys."

He leaned closer to her. "How about I cook us up some breakfast."

"Out of European shows?" she teased.

He chuckled, the deep sound sending more waves of desire through her. "No, I could do this for hours. But since I didn't get a chance to eat any of the dinner I cooked last night…"

"What?" She frowned. "None of it?" Sympathy spiked through her mind.

He shrugged. "Samples, but not a full meal's worth."

"I guess I could eat." She stood up. "Can I help?"

He laughed.

"What?" She turned towards him, her hands on her hips. "I can cook." She crossed her arms over her chest when he just raised his eyebrows as his eyes roamed over her slowly.

"We shall see," he said slowly, then walked over and handed her a crisp white apron.

She wanted nothing more than to wipe that smirk off his face and spent the next thirty minutes impressing him with her skill at making scrambled eggs and fresh homemade biscuits with cream gravy. He sat across the room from her and watched her every move. She could tell he was itching to dive in and help, but he stopped himself from doing so.

"It's a southern thing," she said when she set the plate in front of him. He frowned up at her. "Trust me."

"I've had biscuits and gravy before," he added.

"Good, then you'll have a comparison for mine." She sat down next to him and waited as he picked up his fork.

She held her breath as he took the first bite. His eyes slid closed. She watched his face for any emotion but saw none. It was driving her freaking nuts.

"Well?" she finally said after a few moments.

"It's…"

"Awesome? Fantastic? The best thing you've eaten all day?" she supplied with a smile.

He chuckled at the last. "I'll give you that one." He took another bite and smiled. "Impressive."

She waited. "Impressive as… in a good thing?"

He slowly nodded. "You're killing me!" she growled out.

He glanced over at her, his plate forgotten. "Now you know what you've been doing to me for the past six months."

She felt her throat tighten. She was saved from answering when the kitchen door swung open and the two officers that had visited them earlier walked in.

"Sorry for interrupting," the older man said, glancing down at the pan of fresh biscuits. "Are those… fresh baked biscuits?" he asked, as he set a large box down on the table.

Lilith swallowed the boulder in her throat and smiled

at the men. "Yes, would you like some?" Even to her, her voice sounded funny.

"We wouldn't want to impose…" the younger man said.

"Nonsense join us." Adam waved them both to stools. "It's the least we can do, especially since it appears you've returned our missing wine."

He walked over and glanced in the box. "We've matched these with the serial numbers you sent over," the older man said, shoveling the first bite of food into his mouth. "Woo wee." He leaned back. "They have a kick. I love it." He leaned in and ate more.

"It's the jalapenos," she supplied as she walked over and peeked into the box.

Adam turned to her. "Jalapenos?"

"Hmm. Sure. It gives the gravy a kick, something to linger." She pulled out a bottle and sighed. "So, maybe we won't have to tell Sarah about this after all." She turned to Adam.

"There is still the matter of the broken bottles."

She frowned and groaned. "I forgot about those."

CHAPTER 3

$\mathcal{L}$ilith was sure she was going to lose her mind.
Sarah had only been gone for three days. Yet she
found herself itching to pick up the phone and
call her back to help deal with the mess. Sure, she'd been
in worse pickles, but knowing that didn't help the current
situation.

Besides, she wasn't any good at lying or hiding things
from her best friend. And she wasn't ready to tell Sarah
about the break-in a few days ago. Or the second kiss
Adam had laid on her.

A kiss that had been so different than the first quick
one he'd given to her out of anger. This one had been
softer and full of desire. She felt her heart kick up a notch
and tried to stay focused.

The longer she put off talking to Sarah, the better, so
she had to suck it up and learn to deal with the problems
herself.

Just then the man's voice on the other end of the phone

broke into her thoughts, giving her the unwelcome news about a late delivery.

"What do you mean you can't have the delivery here until Thursday?" she growled into the phone, then listened as the general manager of their local produce supplier explained how they had lost their last shipment. "I don't care what you need to do, just have our order to us by tomorrow afternoon." She slammed down the phone and cringed when she realized that even if the delivery did come tomorrow afternoon, she was still going to have to explain to Adam that his order was going to be late.

She'd avoided him ever since the other morning. It hadn't been hard, really. She'd been rushing around dealing with running East Haven and hadn't stopped long enough to think about how the man made her feel.

But knowing she had to deliver the bad news to him personally made her knees a little wobbly. Not that she was afraid of how he'd take the news, but of what just seeing his blue eyes looking back at her did to her body.

She avoided heading down to the kitchen for as long as she could, but less than an hour later found herself standing outside the swinging doors. She could hear him inside, yelling at one of his crew in French, even though only two of them spoke the language fluently.

Taking a deep breath, she pushed open the door and stepped into the busiest room in the resort. She had purposely picked this time of day to deal with Adam since she knew he'd be too busy to argue with her.

Her eyes moved over to where he stood at the cook's table, wiping the sides of a dish that was about to be served. She'd spent enough time in the dining room delivering food that she knew he demanded nothing but perfection when it came to the look and taste of his meals. And, she had to admit, he was good at it.

Adam was too busy to notice her, which was to her benefit. She moved quickly until she stood directly behind him.

"The produce order won't be here until tomorrow," she blurted out quickly. When she turned to leave, he grabbed her arm and pulled her towards the back office. Dragging her heels would have been a waste of time, so she allowed him to lead her into his office.

When the door shut behind her, she opened her mouth for what she assumed would be an argument, only to have her shoulders pushed against the door and her mouth covered greedily with his.

When his lips slanted over hers, she couldn't stop her body from melting against his. Almost as quickly as the kiss started, he broke away.

"What the hell do you mean my produce won't be here until tomorrow?" He took a step back, then ran his fingers through his hair as he began to pace inside the small room. "As it is, I'm already low." He dropped his hand and turned towards her. "There isn't even enough for the anniversary party tonight." It almost came out as a growl.

"Um." Her mind was still a little too foggy from the kiss to really understand what he was saying.

Instead of waiting for her to reply, he continued to complain. At one point, he switched to French and she almost let a chuckle escape her lips. Finally, when he'd run out of words, he turned back to her.

"Well?" He waited.

She bit her bottom lip and wished more than anything

she had been paying attention to what he was saying, instead of how sexy he looked in his uniform.

"Um," she repeated, causing him to growl and move closer to her.

"Can you or can't you?"

"I…" Sighing, she crossed her arms over her chest. "Maybe if you would say it again in English this time, I could answer you."

She saw him sway a little like she'd slapped him. His chin dropped slightly and he shook his head. "If I give you a list of items I'm low on, can you run into town and get them from the store yourself?"

"I have a few things to deal with first, but I see no reason why I couldn't make a quick trip." This was going better than she'd imagined it would.

He turned away from her, sat behind his desk, and started writing on a pad of paper.

When he handed her the paper, she quickly tucked it into her slacks pocket and turned to go.

"Lilly, we'll have to talk sooner or later." His voice was smooth and rich, and she didn't dare turn to look at him.

Nodding, she quickly disappeared from his office. As she made her way back up the two flights of stairs to Sarah's office, the sound of his voice calling her Lilly played over in her mind.

No one had ever called her Lilly before. Actually, it had taken almost a year for her to get used to being called Lilith, a name she'd picked from an old romance book she'd found on a bus once. She'd always thought it sounded so romantic, so when she'd decided to make the name change, the choice had been obvious.

Sitting behind Sarah's desk, she pulled up the spreadsheet Sarah had left her and checked the schedule. Seeing that there was only the anniversary party scheduled for that evening at the pool veranda, she relaxed a little.

She had a note from Rodney about some plants that had been destroyed during the last group's party. She figured she could swing by and talk to Rodney before she called for Jerry to pick her up at the docks.

Changing out of her dress shoes and slipping on a pair of flats, she grabbed her purse and started downstairs. She ran into several employees on the way down, including one of her newest, Rebecca.

The young woman reminded Lilith so much of herself when she was eighteen. It seemed so long ago now. So much had changed. She'd changed.

Walking outside, she stopped to chat with a few guests. The older couple who would be celebrating their fiftieth anniversary later that night by the pool stopped to thank her for the gift of flowers and champagne that had been delivered to their room earlier that morning.

When she stepped out into the gardens, she couldn't stop the smile from forming on her lips. This was her favorite spot on the island. Here, where the flowers were perfectly maintained, the birds and bees were busy around her, and she could just imagine herself spending the entire day in the warm sun.

"If you stand there too much longer, you'll get sunburned," Rodney's soft voice sounded from beside her. She hadn't heard the old man approach her; she'd been enjoying herself too much.

"Oh, I think my pale skin could tolerate a little color." She smiled and took the single white rose the man offered her each time he saw her. She dipped her nose into the soft petals and enjoyed the sweet scent.

"I suppose so, but still…" He patted her hand. "How's does it feel, boss lady, running the old place all by yourself?"

She giggled. "I think I might survive until Sarah gets back."

"Just survive?" He leaned closer to her and winked. When he started strolling along the pathway, she joined him.

"What's this about some bushes being destroyed?"

"Not destroyed, taken."

She stopped and blinked. "Taken? As in stolen?" Rodney stopped and looked back at her.

"Yup, about ten of them. We'd just planted them earlier that day."

"Saturday?" she asked, feeling her heart skip.

"Nope, Sunday."

"But you don't work Sundays. Or aren't supposed to. Saturdays either."

She thought she saw the old man actually blush before he turned away from her.

"The job needed doing," he said as he continued to walk along the pathway. "Besides, I had to do something to keep my grandson busy. The boy gets into trouble if he doesn't have something to do."

"I thought Nate was doing much better. Especially after the… incident." She didn't want to bring up the fact that a few months back she'd caught the nineteen-year-old stealing from the employees' store.

Since the resort was on a secluded island, they had a large shed that was kept stocked with the basic items that one would need in life. Most of the employees actually lived in the dorm building near the docks full time. Some, like Sarah, split their time between the island and the town of Silver Cove, just across the water on the mainland.

Lilith, for her part, had been living in her dorm room for almost ten years, ever since Sarah had persuaded the old manager, Tom Elliott, to hire her on as a maid.

Since moving in, she'd worked every job possible at East Haven, including one wonderful summer where Rodney had taken her under his wing and taught her to love working in the dirt.

"Oh, he is," Rodney said, breaking into her memories. "It's just best to keep him busy." He turned down the back pathway towards the hidden cottage that only employees knew about. "I seem to remember another young teenager who needed to stay busy too."

She laughed. "You never gave me a moment's rest. Who would have thought there was so much to do to keep all this"—she motioned around them— "beautiful?"

"I'll take that as a compliment," he said, stopping and pointing downwards. "They were sumacs. Red ones. Once they had grown a little, it would have made this whole area look like it was on fire." He sighed and shook his head. "Tis a shame. I'm having to wait three more weeks for others to arrive to replace them."

"Do you have any idea why these would be taken and no others?"

He nodded. "I paid a hundred for each bush since they were larger in size."

"You think someone took them and sold them?"

He shrugged. "What else would they take them for? They're bushes, not bottles of expensive wine."

She cringed inwardly. She'd been torturing herself about not calling or texting Sarah about the break-in but stopping the news from spreading on the island had been another issue. Everyone knew what had happened Saturday night.

"Do you have your receipt? I'm heading into town now and will stop by the police station to report them stolen." She reached into her purse and pulled out her cell phone to snap a few pictures of the empty spots.

"Receipt and a few pictures I took shortly after we were done planting them." He pulled out the receipt from his pocket and handed it to her, then took out his phone. "I'm sending the pictures to you now."

She waited until the three images were received and then followed him back to the main building. "I'll keep you posted."

She sent a text to Jerry to pick her up at the docks and was surprised that he was already there when she walked down to the dock.

"What's it like being the boss?" Jerry teased her. She'd known him for so long, she could tell by just looking at him what sort of mood he was in.

"What's wrong?" She walked onto the ferry and followed him up the stairs.

He glanced back at her with a frown. "My agent called."

"And?"

"They want to make *Crescent Creek* into a movie."

"That's wonderful!" She almost squealed it.

"No, it's not."

"Why not?" She stopped her happy little dance and frowned up at him.

"Because that means I'd have to go to Hollywood."

"For how long?"

"Two months."

"And?"

"You know." He crossed his arms over his chest. She moved closer to him, laying her hands on his arms.

"Jerry, you can do this."

"No, I can't. Not after…" He closed his eyes and sighed. "No, I can't," he repeated.

"What about…" She was interrupted when someone coughed.

She was so surprised by the loud sound, she actually jumped.

Adam stood a few feet away from the pair who were in what could only be described as a tender embrace.

"Sorry to interrupt," he said between clenched teeth. His eyes bore into Lilith's, then Jerry's.

He actually liked the ferryman. The man was his age and roughly the same build. The only difference was that Jerry was three generations American and was one of the bestselling horror authors around. If you didn't count the King.

"No, no interruption." Jerry quickly turned away from Lilith and walked into the small captain's area.

"Did you forget something on your list?" Lilith asked him.

"No," he answered, keeping his eyes glued to hers as pain speared his heart.

He watched her eyebrows raise up slowly. "Then?"

He crossed his arms over his chest. "When were you going to tell me about you two?"

"About…" She blinked and frowned. "Who two?"

Adam nodded towards Jerry, who was busy steering the ferry out of the dock area.

Lilith followed his eyes, then smiled, which turned quickly into a laugh. "Us?" She leaned against the railing. "There is no us." She waved her hand between her and Jerry.

"That's not the way it just appeared."

She tilted her head, then glanced back up at Jerry, who was trying to look very busy. "I suppose…" She crossed her arms over her chest as she thought about it.

"Lilly," he warned as he moved closer to her.

She glanced back at him with a smile. "I was just comforting a friend who was worried about something. That's all."

He felt his heartbeat return to normal. "That's all?"

She smiled and nodded, then crossed her fingers over her purse. Then she frowned. "Now you're stuck…"

His chuckle was quick. "I don't mind." He moved towards her, itching to reach out and touch her auburn hair.

"Going to town." She nodded towards the docks.

Laughing, he turned towards her. "That's why I called Jerry to pick me up."

"But… I thought you wanted…" He watched realization hit her. "You planned this!" It came out more as an accusation than a question.

"But of course." He reached out and tucked a loose strand of her soft hair behind her ear. "How else was I going to get you to talk to me?"

"By kidnapping me?"

"This isn't a kidnapping. You're free to go wherever you wish. Once we dock."

She glared at him for a moment. "What is so important you felt like you had to kidnap me?"

He tilted his head. "I didn't kidnap—" She rolled her eyes, stopping him. He took her hand and walked down the narrow stairs with her until they reached the railing below. "I was hoping we would talk about us."

"There is no us." She leaned against the railing. He waited, just watching her. When she shrugged her shoulders, his lips curved up. "Two kisses don't make an 'us.'"

"Three," he corrected, "and no, I suppose not." He brushed a finger down her shoulders. She was wearing her standard white attire for work, but instead of the spiky heels she had on earlier, she wore flats, which made her almost an entire foot shorter than him. He loved looking into her hazel eyes. Each time he looked, they appeared to be a different color. This time, they were almost sea green, matching the color of the water behind her. "What would you deem 'us' worthy?"

"Oh no." She stood up and shook her head. "I'm not going to go down that path." She walked away, then turned and came back. "This is not happening." She leaned in close. "I can't stand you."

He smiled. "That is good."

She growled lightly. "No, here in the real world, for there to be some sort of relationship, two people have to be able to at least stand one another."

His hand reached out, taking her waist and pulling her close. "I enjoy seeing you worked up."

Her eyes narrowed. "Yes, I can see that. You tend to make me that way all the time."

"Bien, then it's settled." He pulled her closer until her hips met his.

"No," she said slowly. "It's not." Her hands pushed against his chest.

Just then the ferry jerked to a halt. "Now, if you don't mind, I'd like to hurry up and get your groceries, so we can get back to work." She turned and stormed onto the dock.

"She sure does have strong feelings for you," Jerry joked behind him.

"Shut up." He laughed back. "Wait and see."

"What? Your body floating by my ferry in the ocean someday?"

Adam turned to his new friend and frowned. "What's wrong?"

"Hollywood wants to turn my book into a movie." Adam knew that Jerry didn't confide in many people and he counted himself lucky that they had become so close so quickly.

Adam could see the fear in his eyes. "I'll call you later tonight," he said. When Jerry nodded, Adam took off after Lilith.

CHAPTER 4

It was half an hour after the last guest from the anniversary party had disappeared back into the main building that Lilith's phone rang. When she glanced down at the screen, she groaned at Sarah's face smiling back at her.

Heather, the Events Coordinator for East Haven, looked over at her phone. "Sarah?" she asked.

"Yes." She thought about swiping and sending the call to voicemail but knew better. "Guess I better bite the bullet. You got this?" She nodded towards the rest of the cleanup.

"Yes, go." Heather waved her off.

She answered the call and nodded towards Heather, knowing her job was done for the night.

"Hey, Mrs. Rothschild. How goes Maui?"

"Wonderful!" She could hear the excitement in her friend's voice. "We're getting ready to head out to our second luau and I just wanted to check in"— she heard

Ben's voice in the background— "and see how things are going."

"Tell Ben it's no bother. We just finished with Mr. and Mrs. Moore's anniversary party."

"I'm so bummed I missed them. Did you—"

"Yes, I delivered their champagne and flowers first thing."

"Good, what about…"

She heard Ben's voice again. "Stop mothering her. She knows how to run the place. Now come over here and show me how to hula again."

Lilith laughed. "Better go, a wife has to make sure she entertains her husband. Besides, everything is running smoothly." She bit her bottom lip and willed the stress in her voice to disappear.

Toeing off her work shoes, she sunk her feet into the soft sand of the beach and sighed.

"I'll be there in a moment," Sarah said to Ben. "What's the sigh for? Is there anything wrong?"

"Nope, just soaking my feet at the beach." She closed her eyes and rolled her shoulders. "Go, enjoy your time and don't worry about us. I've got everything under control."

"Was there something out of control?" Sarah asked.

"Will you stop." She laughed. "I'm hanging up now…" She waited.

"Okay," Sarah said after a moment. "I'm going. But if you need—"

She clicked off her phone and laughed. "You owe me one, Ben," she said into the night air.

Her feet tingled where the cool water rushed around them. She normally didn't wear heels all day long, since her job usually had her rushing around. But she figured since she was in charge, she had better look the part. Besides, Sarah was always wearing heels and she figured if her friend could do it, so could she.

Now, however, she was finding it impossible to consider sliding her sore feet back into the heels she'd tossed into the sand a few feet away. Tucking her phone into her pocket, she leaned down and rolled her pant legs up then waded into the water a little further.

She glanced up at the sky, which was filled with bright stars. It was one of the main reasons the private beach area was one of the most popular spots on the island.

But since all of the guests had been at the party and were now tucked safely inside the resort, she had the beach all to herself.

She felt her body sway with the wind as her mind rushed back to the conversation she'd had with Adam as they had shopped. From the sounds of it, he enjoyed pissing her off and acted like it was all part of the normal pre-dating ritual.

Just the fact that he thought she'd date him made her laugh. Adam Carriveau was one of the most arrogant, annoying, self-centered… She took a deep breath when she felt her entire body tense. The fact that Adam was trying to have any relationship with her was one of the funniest jokes she'd heard all year.

She didn't do relationships. Well, romantic ones, at any rate. The fact that she was quickly approaching her twenty-fourth birthday and hadn't had any serious boyfriends suited her just fine. Sure, there had been a few guys she'd gone out with, but nothing that had lasted longer than a couple dates and some sweet kisses.

Nope, she was happy with everything just the way it was.

She was turning around to head back towards the pool area to see if Heather needed any more help when she saw a movement out of the corner of her eye. Spinning around, she jerked fast enough to stub her toe on a very large rock and started to fall forward. Reaching out, she tried to right herself before doing a face-plant into ankle-deep water, when two large hands reached out and gripped her hips and set her gently down in the soft sand.

"You okay?" Adam said, laughing down at her.

"Yes. Fine." She jerked her hands away from him. "Didn't anyone ever tell you it was rude to sneak up on someone?" She crossed her arms over her chest and glared at him.

It was a little too dark to see his face, but she could just imagine him smiling back at her. Which only made her angrier.

His chuckle made it worse. "I didn't sneak up. Actually, I… never mind." He leaned down to pick up a few rocks, then slowly tossed them into the water.

Her heart had just returned to its normal pace and she was beginning to realize that she'd been so lost in her thoughts that she wouldn't have heard a tow truck backing up behind her.

Closing her eyes, she took a deep breath. "Sorry, I guess I'm just a little jumpy."

"A little?" He glanced over at her.

"Trying to piss me off again?" she warned, only to have him laugh at her.

"I did establish that I enjoy it, oui." He tossed another stone.

"Why are you out here?" she said through clenched teeth.

"Heather said you had come this way." He shrugged his shoulders. "I figured I could use a walk myself." He turned towards her. "How did your call with Sarah go?"

"Great." She walked over and sat down in the soft sand.

"Did you tell her about the break-in?" He sat next to her, his knee brushing up against her own.

"No." She bit her bottom lip and looked out at the dark water. "It didn't come up."

"She'll find out sooner or later."

"I suppose, but for now she's enjoying her honeymoon."

"Bien. As she should." He leaned back and rested on his elbows. "How did the party go?"

She glanced at him sideways. "Why?"

He smiled. "Because I am interested in how your day went. Isn't this normal 'us' things?"

She rolled her eyes. "You don't have to..." She stopped when he sat up.

"Quelle?"

Shaking her head, she rested back and told him how the party went. If he really wanted to sit and listen to her go on about her boring day, she would give him every little detail.

Adam had never been so entertained in all his life.

Sure, for the most part, he was ignoring every word she said, but he was totally mesmerized by her mouth. The small dimple on the left side of her lips was intoxicating. When she worried about something, her bottom lip would push out in an almost-pout and a small crease would appear between her eyebrows.

Not to mention how she waved her hands around when she spoke. It was all very entertaining.

He could sit in the cool sand all night and listen to her talk until the sun came up. But when he noticed her shiver for the second time, he decided they needed to head back inside.

Standing up, he reached for her and helped her to her feet. "I'm sorry if I startled you," he said as his hands wrapped around her tiny waist.

"It wasn't really your fault. I was deep in thought." Her body relaxed next to his and he felt his body react instantly.

"I wish to kiss you again," he said softly. He waited until he saw a slight smile on her lips before leaning down to cover those sexy lips with his own.

She tasted like berries. Her plump bottom lip pushed up against his, causing his mind to flood with a million different desires. His fingers bunched the hem of her top up as his tongue darted in to explore her sweet mouth.

He heard a light moan escape her lips when he shifted her. When her fingers dug into his shoulders, he wished more than anything that he could put all caution away and take her here and now.

"You've been driving me crazy," he whispered next to her ear. He nibbled on the lobe and tasted the skin on her neck. "Je te veux," he whispered over her skin.

"Don't." Her voice was weak, but her hands pushed him away. "I… I don't think. I'm not…" She took a deep breath. "I'm not looking for relationships." Her chin went up slightly.

"Pourquoi?" His hands reached out to steady her, but she pushed them away.

"I just… I'm not." She took a step back. "Sorry." She turned and walked over to where her shoes were and then disappeared down the pathway.

It took him a moment to gather his thoughts, but then he took a few cleansing breaths and followed her back to the dorms, making sure she arrived safely to her own room before storming into his own, just down the hallway.

He had shut the door and tossed his shirt on the bed when he heard the scream.

He was down the hallway and gathering Lilith up in his arms before the scream had finished leaving her lips.

"What?" he asked, but looking over her head, he noticed what the problem was.

Her room looked like a tornado had gone through it. Each of her drawers were pulled out and thrown on the floor. Clothes were tossed everywhere, and her desk was turned upside down. He could see what appeared to be her laptop, smashed into pieces.

"I…" She cried against his shoulder.

"What's going on?" Heather asked behind him.

"Call the police. Someone's broken into Lilly's room," he told her.

"Wow! Sure," she said. More and more people came out into the hallway to see what was going on. Without questioning it, he lifted Lilly into his arms and carried her past the growing crowd towards his room.

"You okay?" he asked, after setting her down on the bed.

"I…" She closed her eyes and took several deep breaths. "I didn't turn on the light right away. I should have… there could have been someone in there." She sat up a little and he watched her eyes go huge. "There still could be."

"No, it was empty." He sat next to her and took her hand in his and watched her eyes slide shut again.

"Who would want to go through my stuff?" she asked under her breath. "It's not like I have anything. Just my laptop, which they probably took." She groaned.

"It's still there, but I'm afraid it was broken," he said, causing her to groan again.

"Who would do this?"

"I'm not sure, but we caught one thief, maybe we can put our heads together and do it again."

The look in her eyes changed from fear to interest. She sat up a little and nodded. "We'll need to find out who's here." She glanced towards his open door. "Don't criminals usually return to the scene?"

He nodded quickly, then without a word, walked out of the room to assess everyone who stood in the hallway.

There were employees he knew lived on the floor below them shuffling into the small hallway. Everyone was trying to get a glance at Lilly's room and talking in low tones.

"Did you call the police?" he asked Heather.

"How is she?" She nodded towards his room.

His eyes moved towards his door. "Shaken."

"I can stay with her if you want."

"No, I've got her. I just wanted to make sure you called."

"Yes, it might be a while. They have to cross on the ferry."

He nodded. "We'll be in there when they arrive."

"I'll let them know."

"Oh, Heather, see if we can keep this away from the guests."

"Of course." She turned and clapped her hands.

"Alright, everyone. We can't do anything else until the police arrive. Let's all go back to our rooms."

He walked back into his room. Lilly had taken his notepad from his desk and was sitting at the edge of the bed, writing names as she peeked out the door.

"Sounds like she has it under control," Lilly said, biting her bottom lip. He could still see the fear, but it was outweighed by determination. "Who am I missing?" She handed him the pad and he jotted a few more names down. When he handed her the list again, she looked over it. "So, pretty much everyone who works on the island is in the hall-way." She frowned and leaned back against his headboard.

He walked over and sat next to her. "Lilly are you okay?" He took the list from her and set it down on the edge of the bed, then once again took her hand in his.

"Yes," she said, but he felt her handshake in his. "Who would want to do this to me?" She rolled her shoulders.

"Well, we have about half an hour before the police get here; let's go through the list." He knew it might keep her mind occupied, so he picked up the list again and started at the top.

By the time the same two officers from the other night knocked on his door, they had narrowed the list down to two people.

"Evening." The younger man, he now knew as Carl, leaned against the door jam. "Heard you had some more trouble out here."

Adam stood up and reached down for Lilly's hand. When she stood, she tucked her hands into her pockets.

"Yes." She glanced at him and he noticed her eyes move over his chest. That was the first time he noticed that he had yet to put back on his shirt. Quickly grabbing his shirt, he pulled it over his head and followed them down the hallway towards her room.

For the next half an hour, she answered every question they had. He even had to answer a few once they realized he'd been the last one to be with her before discovering her room.

Heather was there as well and confirmed that she'd returned only a few minutes before they had. She hadn't seen anyone or anything, which left them knocking on all the other employees' doors to have them answer the same questions. The hour dragged on and by the time the police left, he could see that Lilly was completely drained.

"Why don't you bunk with me tonight?" Heather chimed in. "Then we can worry about cleaning up tomorrow." She wrapped her arm around Lilly's shoulders.

"I… yes, that would be great." He watched Lilly's eyes dart towards her own door.

"Do you need anything?" He stepped forward.

"No." She shook her head. "I was just wondering if it would be terrible if I just burned everything in there." He saw her shiver.

"Come on, we'll think about it tomorrow." Heather ushered her towards her own door near the end of the hallway.

He watched the pair disappear, then turned towards her room and stepped into the darkness. He wasn't done looking around. There had to be a clue somewhere as to who did this and why. Somewhere in this mess was the key to helping him protect the woman he was quickly falling in love with.

CHAPTER 5

It was almost too much for her to handle. Lilith sat on the edge of her bed and fought back the tears.

This small room had been the only home that had ever meant anything to her. And now… it felt violated.

She didn't even want her favorite pair of sneakers, laying just outside her closet doors, let alone the clothes that had been tossed around the room.

She was thankful Adam had been there last night but grateful that Heather offered to let her stay with her. It had taken all her willpower not to focus on Adam's bare chest as they waited for the police to arrive.

At least focusing on him had taken her mind off of… this. She glanced around the destroyed room, not knowing where to start.

She had a handful of trash bags and started tossing everything she could into them. She planned on donating everything in town. Whoever had done this had touched everything, including, from the looks of it, eighty percent of her clothes.

When she glanced at the clock, she realized she had just under an hour before the first event of the day, a birthday party on the back lawn.

Heather had assured her that they could handle it without her, but since she was ninety percent done, she figured she'd shower and get dressed so she could help out.

When she walked down the stairs thirty minutes later, dressed in the same clothes she'd worn the day before, she was greeted by Heather.

"Nope!" Her friend crossed her arms over her chest. "You'd better head right back up those stairs."

"I'm just going—"

"Going to head back upstairs," Heather supplied.

"No. I'm done upstairs." She sighed. "I need something to take my mind off… things."

"What about a day on the mainland?" Heather suggested. "We really do have things under control here. Besides, something tells me you need to spend your last paycheck on some new clothes." She nodded to her outfit.

Lilith looked down and sighed. "Yes, I could use some new things." She thought about the mental list she'd made upstairs.

"Then go. Today we don't need you, but tomorrow…" She rolled her eyes. "No skipping out."

"The Tanner party." She groaned. "Okay, I'm heading out now, but only because I can't wear this"—she tapped her pants— "tomorrow."

"Good." Heather turned to go. "Oh, and while you're

at it, do something nice for yourself. You deserve it." With that, her friend was gone.

Heather was a recent addition to East Haven. She'd only been there for a little over a year, but since arriving, the woman had been invaluable. Sarah had quickly promoted her to Events Coordinator.

Not a lot of people knew the woman's past or where she'd come from, but Lilith had an in with the boss and had quickly become friends with the woman. Heather was a divorcee. Two times over. It was hard to believe, but Heather actually believed that she was addicted to marriage. Weddings, to be exact. Or so she said.

So, she'd decided that instead of picking husband number three, she'd arrange and enjoy other people's special days.

The fact that they were the same age shocked her. She couldn't imagine being married once at her age, let alone twice.

Heading back upstairs to gather her purse and the donation bags, she bumped solidly into Nate, Rodney's grandson.

"Sorry." She gripped the railing to keep from falling backward as his hands wrapped around her waist.

"Oops," he said and she instantly smelled cigarettes on his breath. She knew that Sarah had already reprimanded him for smoking outside of designated areas, in addition to a few other reasons. "Guess I better watch where I'm heading." He chuckled, not releasing her.

The kid was tall, and when you added the fact that he was a step above her, she had to crank her neck back just to look up at him.

"No problem." She started to step down and away, but he only tightened his grip on her.

His blond hair somehow always looked greasy and was tied back with a thick leather strap. His blue eyes laughed at her as she tried once more to move away.

"Nate, I'm not going to fall backward. You can let go of me now."

"Are you sure you want me to?" His blue eyes roamed over her. "I heard there were some problems at your place last night."

She tensed. "Yes, someone broke in."

His eyes grew darker. "They didn't hurt you, did they?"

"No." She smiled. "I wasn't there."

"Good." He nodded and dropped his hands. "Well, if you need someone to…" He dropped off.

"I'll be fine. Thank you." She moved aside and leaned against the wall as he stepped past her. She noticed that the sun had cleared up his pimpled face a little.

She wondered if the kid would ever have clear skin and thought about suggesting some products that would help but bit her tongue instead.

She'd struggled when she'd been in her early teens. Thankfully, Sarah's mother, Crystal, had shown her a homemade remedy that had cleared up her face. She still used the stuff. Which reminded her that she'd have to make a stop at Serenity's Attic, Crystal's store in town, to get some more since her bottle had been smashed in last night's break-in.

"Well, like I said if you need someone…" His eyes moved over her again and she felt a shiver run up her spine.

"Thanks." She waited until he disappeared down the hallway.

By the time she walked her old bike off the ferry and rode into town, she had a long list of things she needed. Deciding the best place to start would be Serenity's Attic, she rode the quarter of a mile into Silver Cove and parked her bike in front of the hippie store.

She just loved this place. Most of the places in town looked the same. Boring. But Serenity's Attic was candy for the eyes with bright colors, designs, and lights covering every inch of the outside.

When she stepped into the shop, a bell rang overhead and she couldn't stop the smile as the smells hit her. Here, too, her senses were entertained. Everything from vanilla to jasmine.

"Lilith." Crystal rushed out from behind the counter, her long hair and dress flowing around her. "Carl was in here earlier and told me about what happened." She was wrapped in a tight hug. "Are you okay?" The woman smelled better than her store and it felt so great to be wrapped in her motherly arms.

Sarah's mother could have easily been on the cover of any popular magazine. Clean, hippie living had made Crystal look more like Sarah's sister. Lilith hoped she would look that good when she hit her forties. Her skin was flawless, and she was sure there wasn't a wrinkle on the woman's body, nor an ounce of fat. Crystal taught the local yoga classes, which could account for the toned muscles holding her now.

"I'm fine. Really. Just desperate to replace everything I own." She slumped her shoulders slightly.

"Well, then you've come to the right place. Sarah has

four boxes of things she was going to have me donate. You're welcome to go through them. If you want."

"Really?" She thought about being able to hold onto most of her paycheck to help pay for the replacement laptop she knew she had to buy. "That would be great."

"Good, the boxes are still in her rooms. You're welcome to head over there. If you need, Rowan can deliver whatever you want." She nodded out towards her bike.

"Again, thank you." She hugged the woman again.

"That's what family does." Crystal patted her back. "Now, what else do you need?"

Fifteen minutes later, Lilith pulled her bike up to the huge house a few blocks away. She parked her bike and frowned down at the large box of items she'd gotten for a steal. Obviously, Crystal had given her the family discount, since the things she'd purchased would have normally run her in the hundreds, but she'd walked out for a little over fifty dollars.

Which had, of course, made her eyes water the entire trip to Crystal and Sarah's house. The place had been in their family for generations and was one of the best and biggest homes in Silver Cove.

Some people in town speculated that the old place was haunted, but Lilith knew better since she'd spent her first year in Silver Cove living under the roof.

Walking up the stairs, she reached for the handle, only to have it yanked open.

"My aunt called." Rowan frowned down at her as his eyes ran over her slowly. "You okay?" He took her shoulders and pulled her into a hug.

"Yes," she said against his chest and felt a tear slide down her nose. "Really. It was just my stuff."

He pulled back and looked into her eyes. "Do you think…" He dropped off his sentence, then glanced around outside and quickly pulled her into the foyer, shutting the massive front door behind him. "Do you think that it could be someone from your past?"

Her heart literally did a flip. She hadn't even thought of that possibility. She felt her breathing hitch and then she was once again being carried.

"Hey." She heard Rowan's voice at the end of the tunnel. "Easy, breathe." He set her down on the sofa and pushed her head between her knees. "Slow. Easy slow breaths."

Closing her eyes, she followed his instructions.

"I didn't mean to scare you," he said after she'd gotten her breathing and heart back to a normal rate.

Shaking her head, she leaned back and rested against the soft cushions. "No, I should have thought…"

"I suppose it's not possible."

"No," she agreed. "Not possible."

"It was probably someone just looking for some stuff to fence," he added. His hand was brushing her shoulder, trying to get her to relax, but it was doing the opposite.

Standing up, she wrapped her arms around herself and walked over to the massive fireplace. The hearth was empty now, but she could close her eyes and remember the warmth she'd felt that first night so many years ago. The first time she'd ever felt the kindness of another human.

"It can't be," she whispered, praying it was the truth.

❅

Adam watched Lilly get out of Rowan's car and felt his shoulders slump. He'd never worked so hard to gain the attention of a woman before. Nor had he ever felt the pain he felt now, seeing the other man help her out of his car, holding her hand and taking her into a light hug.

He tried to tell himself it was just a brotherly hug, but his jealousy got the better of him and he flew across the yard towards the couple.

"I'm sure I can carry everything..." Lilly was saying as he approached.

"Are you okay, Lilly?" Adam broke in as he stopped a foot from the other man, who instantly took a step back.

"I'm fine," Lilly answered as she frowned at him. "Rowan was just helping me—"

"Heather said you went into town. You should have let me know—"

"So you could what?" She crossed her arms over her chest. "Skip out on work and go clothes shopping with me?"

He cringed then glanced at Rowan, who just smiled and shrugged at him like he wasn't going to offer any help. "I'll just get those boxes out of my trunk." Rowan disappeared behind his car.

"I was worried about you." He moved closer and placed his hands gently on her shoulders. He saw her eyes turn soft.

"I'm fine. Especially since I have a whole new wardrobe and all new toiletries." Her smile grew. "Now if my fairy godmother would zap me a new Mac, I'd be in heaven."

"I don't know about anything new, but I have an old PC you can borrow." She cringed at his offer.

"I'm kind of a Mac person."

He laughed. "Sorry, maybe it will do until you can find a replacement."

"I'll take it." She turned to Rowan, then glanced back at him. "Now, who wants to help me carry all these upstairs?"

"I'll help you carry them, but the dinner rush is about to start, so you'll have to unload them all yourself." He walked over and took a box from Rowan's trunk. "Thanks," he whispered to the other man.

"Anytime." He nodded back. "I can help. I'm not on shift at the hospital until ten."

"I thought you were opening your own clinic?" Lilith asked as she walked over and took a large brown bag from the trunk.

"I am; the doors open next month. Until then, I'm volunteering at the hospital in Freeport." Rowan shifted a box so he could add another to his arms.

Suddenly Adam felt like an underachiever. He knew he was doing what he was meant to in life, but still, he heard his father's voice in the back of his mind, nagging at him. His entire body tensed, and he felt his jaw tighten.

Then Lilly's hand rested on his arms and his mind went blank. "Thanks for helping." It came out as a whisper and he could see she was still fighting off the tears. He figured no words were needed. Especially since he didn't know what to say and didn't think he could handle seeing her eyes fill with hurt and pain again if he said the wrong thing.

He helped Rowan carry several boxes up to her room. She had cleared everything out, including the broken chair. When he walked back into the kitchen, he felt a little more settled. Maybe it was because he knew Lilly was up in her room happily unpacking, or maybe it was because she'd shown a hint of kindness towards him for the first time. Either way, that evening's shift seemed to fly by.

On his way back to his room, he stopped by and, seeing the light under her door, he knocked.

When she opened the door, he felt his mouth water. Her hair was piled on top of her head in a messy bun, and several strands had fallen loose around her face. She was wearing a pair of gray sweat shorts and an old Boston University T-shirt that looked like it had spent too much time in the wash.

"Hey," she said, leaning against her door. "How'd dinner go?"

"Fine." His eyes roamed behind her, surprised that she still had plenty of unpacking to do.

"Need some help?" He nodded towards a large pile of clothes that currently took up her entire bed.

"No, I…" She glanced around, then blew a wisp of hair out of her eyes. "Yes," she groaned. "Tons of it." Her shoulders sagged. She stood aside and he walked in. "Heather has the wine social this evening and I'm desperate," she explained.

"It doesn't seem that hard to me, you just take those empty hangers there and…" He walked over as she shut her door and leaned against it, then he picked up a black hanger, slid a dress over, and held it up. "Voilà."

She glared at him. "It's not that simple."

"No?" He walked over and hung the dress up in her almost empty closet.

"No." She followed him and took the dress down.

"First, I have to decide if it fits. Then I have to decide if it fits me."

"Aren't those the same thing?"

She chuckled. "For a Frenchman, you sure know nothing about fashion."

"It seems easy enough. Try it on, if it fits, hang it up." He crossed his arms over his chest. She looked down at the dress in question and frowned.

"I was about to try this one on." Her eyes moved up to his. He held in a smile and only raised his eyebrows up slightly.

"Well…"

She tilted her head. "There is no way I'm going to change with you in the room."

"So, change in the bathroom."

She glanced towards the bathroom door, then back at him. "It would be nice to have a second opinion. I'm so terrible at this. Usually, I take Sarah or Heather with me." She bit her bottom lip.

"So, use me instead." He walked over to the oversized chair in the corner of her room and sat down. "Go ahead. I've nothing better to do."

She walked over to the bed and picked up a handful of clothes. "But I want your honest opinions."

"But of course." He added the thick French accent to the statement.

She hesitated just outside the bathroom door, then walked over to the closet where she'd hung a dozen other items and grabbed those too. "I never go shopping without Sarah," she growled and disappeared into the bathroom.

Less than two minutes later, she walked out and he felt his mouth water again.

"You're not saying anything." She frowned and glanced down at the dress. "I thought I really liked—"

Before his mind could catch up with his body, he was across the room and had her in his arms. His mouth covered hers, quickly ending her sentence.

He felt her tense body melt against his as his tongue played over her lips. "Keep the dress," he said softly when he moved away.

"Well, if it gets this kind of response, I think it should be kept under lock and key," she joked as his hands ran up and down her sides.

"You should wear this one evening and I'll take you to dinner on the mainland."

He felt her tense and lean back. "Was that an offer to go out on a date?"

He shrugged. "It is if the answer is yes."

Her eyes roamed over his face and she bit her bottom lip again, making him wish he could lean closer and take over for her at the task.

"Maybe when Sarah and Ben get back." She took a step back. "Until then I'm way too busy." She sighed and turned back to the bathroom and a low growl released from his chest.

She stopped and turned around, then smiled. "I like the back too."

As she walked into the bathroom, he stared at her bare back and knew the rest of the evening was going to be pure torture on his libido.

CHAPTER 6

The next day was too busy for Lilith to remember. Guests left and a whole new group arrived. The party of almost fifty would occupy the entire island all weekend. The fact that it was one of the most prestigious families in the States didn't faze her or any of the employees at East Haven. What did faze them was the fact that they were known to be one of the most demanding.

Before the private yachts started arriving, Lilith met with all of the employees to run over a few items. Of course, she had started in the kitchen. Adam leaned against the wall and acted like he was annoyed at her talking to his crew. But she pushed through her planned speech anyway and was halfway through before she felt her body relax.

"Remember the old adage, the customer is always right. With the Robinsons, we're going to take that statement one step further. There should never be a need for a customer to have to make a request. Meaning..." She glanced around the kitchen and noticed everyone was listening. "Eyes and ears should be open. If you see a glass half full, fill it before someone has to glance around to hunt you down. If you hear someone complain about something, make it right. If you can't do so, page me immediately." She noticed a few people glancing towards one server in particular. "If you need to step out for a smoke break, make sure someone else will be watching your tables."

She waited a moment, then turned away from the wait staff. "I trust Adam will make sure everything leaving the kitchen is perfect." She glanced over at him and thought she saw the side of his lips curve upward, but as soon as it happened, it was gone. "That is all." She turned to go and made it just outside the door before Adam caught up with her.

"Pretty motivating speech." He fell into step beside her as she made her way through the dining hall.

"Thanks."

"So…" He took her arm to stop her before she ascended the large staircase that split the building in half. It was one of the most charming parts of the resort. The intricate wood railing dated back centuries. Its dark runner had recently been replaced, giving the stairs a fresh look. "I was thinking about next Tuesday night."

Her eyebrows rose in question.

"For our date." His fingers brushed over her bare arm, causing her entire body to respond.

"Date?" She blinked as her mind went blank. His eyes pierced her, and she remembered the kiss the night before. When her knees started to buckle, she reached out and took hold of the oak banister to steady herself.

"Sure." He lowered his voice and moved closer. "I

figured you could wear that dress"—his eyes flickered down her body— "and we could get to know one another."

She giggled. She couldn't help it. "Is that the best line you have?" She took a step back, needing the air and a moment to compose herself.

His smile was quick. "I have plenty more." He relaxed against the railing. "How about after the dinner rush, we head out?"

She nodded, still smiling, and then turned and started making her way up the stairs. "Oh, and Adam?" She stopped and glanced over her shoulder. "Make sure everything coming out of the kitchen is perfect this weekend." There, she saw the old temper flare in his eyes and smiled even bigger as she made her way towards Sarah's office to meet with the rest of the staff.

Two hours after the entire Robinson clan arrived, her head was splitting, and she was wondering how she and the staff were going to make it through the rest of the weekend.

Sarah had called her twice already and even though she knew her friend only meant to help, she quickly switched off her phone, so she wouldn't be distracted again.

Her radio pipped in her ear so much she had to turn it down. For the next few hours, she handled every complaint. Beds were too hard, pillows too soft, rooms didn't have the best view and had to be switched, luggage had been scuffed. And all this before most of the guests had even been checked in. She knew that it truly was going to be the weekend from hell.

Just before dinner, she ran into a group of men standing on the balcony smoking. There were several signs posted, leading the smokers away from the main building, but the group was clearly ignoring them. Deciding quickly how to best handle the situation, she walked over to the group.

"Beautiful evening isn't it?" She leaned against the railing.

"It's okay," two of the men replied.

A tall blond man quickly flicked his cigarette out into the yard and she felt her back teeth clench as she made a mental note to pick up the butt. "Your name is Lilith?" he said as he leaned next to her and ran a finger over her nametag.

"Yes, I'm the general manager in charge. I hope you're finding everything here at East Haven to your pleasing."

The blond leaned closer. "I'm Tristen Robinson."

The name was familiar, as was the face. But she didn't let that affect her. The fact that he was one of the most eligible bachelors in New York meant little to her.

"Yes, it's my job to know everyone here." She smiled and decided to quickly get them to move towards the designated smoking area. "Have you discovered the pavilion yet? It's our designated smoking area and the view of the ocean is spectacular from there."

"No." His hand reached out to brush her arm. She straightened. "I would be willing to show you gentlemen the area." She waited.

"We were done anyway." The other two flicked their cigarettes into the yard and she tried not to show her anger. Then they turned and left her alone with Tristen.

Instantly, she was rethinking her tactics and took a step back.

"So…" He leaned closer to her once more. "Why don't

you show me that spot." His fingers trailed up her arm, causing her to shiver.

"I'd be happy to, but I just remembered—" She stopped when he laughed.

"Afraid to be left alone with me?" he teased, causing her chin to rise.

"Of course not, Mr. Robinson."

This time his laughter sounded sincerer. "Tristen. No one and I do mean no one, calls me Mr. Robinson."

She nodded quickly. "I'm not afraid. We are coming up on dinner and I have things to see to." She took a step back and he frowned as his hand dropped away from her bare skin. "If you would, please make sure you find your way towards the pavilion for your next smoke break." She motioned. "There are signs leading you down the pathway."

He smiled as he leaned back against the railing. "You're a stickler for rules, aren't you?"

"It's my job." She started to move away.

"How long have you been at it?" he broke in, stopping her from walking away. Another rule of the trade never leave a guest who has questions.

"I've worked at East Haven for over nine years."

He whistled. "That's a long time. What'd you do? Start when you were fifteen?"

"Sixteen," she supplied.

He whistled again, then straightened and moved towards her. "I'd like to hear more—"

Her radio chimed in her ear and she reached over to turn it down.

"Maybe later," he added and stepped back as a couple more people walked out onto the porch and lit up.

"Smoking area's down there," he added, pointing to the pathway.

She hid a smile as she turned away and made a quick retreat.

She had a few errands to run outside before heading into the main dining hall. She swung by the pool area and made sure everything was in order for the pool party later that evening.

Then she walked by the pavilion and was surprised to see Tristen and the group of guys he'd been talking to earlier out there relaxing and enjoying their cigarettes.

Turning away before they noticed her, she headed back to the main building. She was walking along the well-lit pathway when she saw the embers of a cigarette and walked off the pathway.

"Nate?" she said, getting the kids attention.

He turned and threw the cigarette out into the trees.

"Hey." He smiled at her and moved closer. "I heard you talking to those guys earlier." He nodded towards the pavilion.

She glanced, then turned back to him. "You know you're not supposed to smoke out here," she started.

"Oh, it's no big deal. I was just finishing up a few things." His hand came up to her arm. "Why don't you take a walk with me? I was just heading to the beach to take a dip." He winked.

"No thank you." She glanced down at her arm and moved away. "I have to get things ready for dinner."

He stepped in front of her, stopping her from walking back onto the pathway.

"Are you sure?" His hand came up and took her arm again. "I'm sure we could have fun together."

Her chin rose. "Nate, I'd hate to mention this conversation to your grandfather after all he's done for you, getting you this job."

She saw anger flood the younger man's eyes, but he took a step back. "The old man is pissing me off. Always making me work."

"That is what I pay you for." She stepped aside easily and left him alone then headed into the main building.

Dinner was chaotic, but the worst moment was when she had to talk Adam down after one of the group complained that his pumpkin ravioli with sage butter was dry. She'd seen the man storm into the dining hall and berate a customer for less before. This time, one of his staff had tipped her off and she'd stopped him before he could enter the dining room.

"Where are you going?" She put her hands against his chest, stopping him. His face was skewed into a frown.

"I'm going to have a talk with someone."

"No, you're not." She felt his muscles under her hands flex and desperately wished to explore the feeling more.

"Pourquoi?" He crossed his arms over his chest and she almost groaned at the feeling of him under her fingers.

"You're needed in the kitchen."

"This…"—she saw him take a deep breath— "naïf vache thinks that my…"

"Yes." She dropped her hands and crossed her arms over her chest. "I heard. Now, let me handle this. Why don't you—"

"No." He moved closer, his face inches from hers, his eyes boring into her. "This is my kitchen, my food. If some ignorant cow has something bad to say…"

"It should be handled by the manager." She stood her

ground. "If you don't like how I deal with it, then I suggest you take it up with Sarah once she returns." She waited and watched him sway back slightly. Just then there was a loud noise from the kitchen. "Now, if you'll excuse me, I'm needing in the dining room and, from the sounds of it, you're needed back in the kitchen."

He glanced back, and she thought she heard him curse in French under his breath as he disappeared back through the doors.

Smiling, she walked into the dining room only to discover that the complaint had come from the table where Tristen sat.

She took a few deep breaths before walking over to his table. There was an older couple sitting with him, along with two women, one of which was hanging on Tristen's arm like she never wanted to let go. The woman looked like she'd stepped directly off a billboard ad. Her long dark locks hung in perfect ringlets over her shoulders.

"Good evening. I hope everything is to your satisfaction." She glanced around the table.

"Yes," the older man said. "We were just talking about how wonderful the meal is." Her eyes moved to Tristen as he set his fork down. His entire plate was cleaned.

"Not me," the woman sitting next to him said. "My food was dry." The woman pushed her barely touched food aside. "I've never tasted something as dry as this. Did the chef dump sand in it?" She pouted. Her hand never left Tristen's arm.

"I apologize. Is there anything else you might prefer?"

"Yes, a new chef," the woman joked, causing several at the table to chuckle.

"I assure you, you are in the best hands. Chef

Carriveau is one of the best in Maine. I'd be happy to bring something else for you to try."

The woman twisted her lips and leaned forward. "If I say I want a new chef, then I'm sure—"

"Don't be a bitch, Kaleen. Why don't you just get the filet mignon? Mine was cooked to perfection," Tristen added. Her eyes moved over to his and he winked at her, causing her to smile.

"Well, if you think it's okay, Trist." She sighed and nodded to Lilith. "I suppose I'll try it."

"I'll see to it myself." She left the table and went back into the kitchen, where Adam was standing between two of his staff members who looked like they had just punched each other.

"What is going on?" She felt her headache triple.

"I'm handling this," Adam growled as he pushed Kenny back a step. "Go, take a walk." He pointed to the door and the man glanced in her direction, then stormed off towards the back door. "Now, do you think you could manage to clean up this mess?" Adam said to Evan, who nodded and went to get a broom to clean up the shattered plates.

She waited until Adam turned to her and relayed the new order, then stood back and watched the kitchen staff work their magic. To her, it was a dance the way they moved around each other, working on their own little tasks, but coming together as one in the end.

By the time the new plate was ready, her headache was pretty much gone. It could have something to do with the fact that Adam had set a plate of sweet potato fries in front of her and she'd munched on them while waiting. Or the fact that just focusing on another person's task had calmed her down.

Either way, when she carried the new meal into the dining room, she had her second wind and knew that she could handle pretty much anything that evening held for her.

Adam usually lived for nights like this, the business of the evening dinner shift. The hustle, the chaos, the noise, and smells of good food cooking. But tonight, he'd had enough. All he could think about was taking a long walk along the beach and then sitting there to watch for falling stars. He imagined he was sitting beside Lilly, holding her, kissing her, and getting to know her. Sure, it was one of the worst lines he'd ever given a woman, but it had never been truer.

He left his staff cleaning up and walked back to his room, showered, changed, and went to find Lilly. He found her in Sarah's office, slumped over a pile of invoices. He stopped just outside the door and watched her peering over a pair of sexy glasses at the paperwork.

"Interesting," he said, causing her to jump slightly. "I didn't know you wore those."

She quickly pulled them off and set them down. "I don't..." When he tilted his head in question, she smiled. "I mean, I don't except when I'm tired, have struggled with a headache all day, and have to pour over invoices late at night."

Without a word, he walked around the desk and took her hand. "I have a cure for all that."

"Oh?" She allowed him to help her stand. He pulled her into his arms.

"Take a walk with me," he said after a moment of silence.

"A walk?" She blinked a few times.

"Sure, I need the fresh air." He stepped back, taking her hand, and started towards the door. She glanced back at the desk with a frown. "Paperwork can wait."

She turned and locked up the office, then followed him down the back stairs and outside. When the cool night air hit him, he sighed. "It never gets old." He closed his eyes and took several deep breaths, then reached down and took her hand in his and started walking towards the back pathway that circled the island.

"I've always loved the air here," he said, glancing down at her.

"Is it different than France?" she asked.

"Some. I don't really remember much about my home-land. I was very small when I moved here."

"How old were you?" she asked.

"Nine."

"Did your parents move here for work?"

"No, my parents are still in France."

She stopped so he turned and looked at her. "Who did you live with then?"

"My grand-mère, Sonya." He smiled, remembering the first time he'd seen the woman's kind face.

"Since you were nine?" she asked.

He nodded, feeling the lump of love in his throat.

"Why? Why didn't you stay with your parents?"

He took her hand, moved to the dock, and sat on the bench that overlooked the boat docks. There were always boats docked there, but now it looked like a millionaire's island. Every boat was a yacht, no doubt some of the most expensive ones to ever be tied up there all at once.

"They sent me to live with my mother's mother to see if she could save me."

"Save you?" Lilly turned towards him, so he wrapped his arm around her shoulders.

"Yes."

"From?"

He shrugged. "I suppose myself. I was a terrible child." He chuckled.

"Still, to send a nine-year-old halfway across the world." She shook her head and he could see the anger cross those lovely eyes of hers.

"Don't be mad. Actually, it's because my Nana raised me that I had the freedom to get where I am today. My father…" He paused and tried to figure out how best to say the next statement. "He's very high up in the government over there. If I had stayed in France, I would have been led down a different path."

She was silent for a while, then leaned back against his arm. "Well, then I'm thankful."

"Oh?" He smiled as his fingers tangled in her hair.

"Yes, it would have been a shame to waste your talent in the kitchen."

He chuckled, and she laughed in response.

"Is that the only reason then?"

She turned and looked up at him. "That's all I can think of." She smiled as his fingers gently ran over her chin, pulling her face up to his.

"Then I'll have to give you more reasons," he said before his lips brushed over hers.

He'd never experienced a kiss that shook him to his core before. He felt like he could spend the rest of his life sitting under the stars, his arms wrapped around Lilly, their lips playing slowly over one another's.

When he pulled away, she rested her head against his shoulder and sighed. He closed his eyes, wishing he could hold onto that moment, wanting to remember it for the rest of his life.

"What about your family?" Instantly he felt her tense and wished he could take his question back.

She sat up, her back straight as her hands gripped her knees. "My folks are out of my life too."

"I'm sorry." He reached over and started to rub her back, but she quickly stood up and walked over to the railing, looking out into the dark night. Moving to stand by her, he waited, watching her facial expressions. "How did they die?" he asked after a moment.

She turned to him. "They didn't," she responded. "I did."

CHAPTER 7

*L*ilith could see the shock and confusion on Adam's face. Taking a deep breath, she closed her eyes and decided that she could trust him with her secret. After all, hadn't he just opened up to her about his life?

"When I was five, my real father died. The only thing I knew about him was that he was in the military and my parents had never married."

"I'm sorry." Adam reached for her, but then dropped his hand instead.

"Shortly after, my mother started dating Dave." She turned away from him, her eyes burning as she looked out into the darkness without seeing anything. "Shortly after he moved in with us, he started sneaking into my room late at night or when my mother was at work."

Adam's hand reached up and took her shoulders gently. "Did he…" She couldn't see his eyes through the mist.

She'd only told three other people in her entire life.

She dipped her chin slightly, and Adam reached up and placed a finger under it until she looked at him directly.

"What happened?"

"It continued until just before my thirteenth birthday."

"Then?"

"Then Hurricane Katrina hit." She took a deep breath. "We lived in a part of town that was quickly under water. Somehow, I got separated from my mother. She had tried to pull me into the rescue boat, but I was sucked under." She closed her eyes, remembering the feeling of drowning, sucking in the water, along with the dirt. Gasping and fighting the strong current. She'd been so thin and frail back then. Her tiny muscles had cramped up and she could remember thinking, "This is it."

The only parts of her life that flashed before her eyes were the terrible ones, so when a hand reached in and grabbed her by the shirt, pulling her to safety, she vowed, with the first real breath in her new life, that she would take control of her own life. No matter what it cost.

"What happened?" Adam asked again.

"Cara Kincaid died that day and Lilith Brown was born. Armed with only what the Red Cross gave me, I hopped on the free bus ride north and stayed in the donated hotels until one night when Crystal, Sarah's mother, offered to put me up. Then, a few weeks into staying with them, I broke down and told them my story."

She sighed and remembered how relieved she'd felt, feeling like she was part of a family for the first time in her life. She and Sarah had quickly become best friends. "Crystal was like the mother I always dreamed of and Sarah the sister I never had. So, they kept me on, and when

I was old enough, I started working here." She turned towards him.

"And no one from your family knows you're alive?"

She shook her head. "No, and I don't know if they survived that day, either. I scoured the news stations and papers, looking for their names, but since my stepfather liked to live off the grid as much as possible, I doubt their names would have shown up on any list. There are still around thirty bodies that haven't been identified..." She dropped her eyes. "I never built up the courage to see..."

"You're better off." He wrapped his arms around her and she felt the tears soak his shirt. "I'm sorry."

"For?" she said against his chest.

She felt his chest rise and fall with his sigh. "Everything. No child should have to bear such abuse. No person should hold in such pain."

She closed her eyes and took in his scent. "I... It's the main reason I'm so scared of relationships." This time she felt him tense.

"Are you... You..." He took another deep breath and she leaned back.

"I haven't been close to anyone before." She watched him drop his arms and take a step back.

"What am I supposed to do with that knowledge?"

She chuckled and shrugged. "I don't know. I've never been in this situation before."

He ran a hand through his hair and walked to the end of the pier, then leaned on the railing and looked out to the night sky.

Walking over, she ran her hands up his arms, feeling the tense muscles in his shoulders. "Adam, I may have kept myself hidden, but with you, I'd like to step back into life. I've kept myself from getting close to a man. I'd like you to be the first one I open up to." She held her breath and waited.

She'd thought long and hard about being with him over the last few days. Actually, she'd fantasized about it for months, ever since she'd seen him step off the ferry for the first time.

"Lilly." He pulled her close. "You are an amazing woman." He rained kisses over her face until he settled over her lips. His hands moved slowly up and down her back. She moaned and pulled him closer.

"Adam…" she said when he pulled back, his head snapping up and his eyes glued to a spot behind her head.

"Shh," he whispered.

"What?" she asked, turning around, looking towards the bushes in question.

"I thought…" He shook his head. "Maybe we should finish our walk."

She sighed, knowing it wouldn't do to have guests discover them the way they had been a few moments ago. Putting her hand in his, she followed him back to the pathway.

"Is your grandmother still alive?"

"Yes, she lives just outside of town. She's as feisty as ever and still has a way of pissing my parents off."

She laughed all of a sudden, causing him to stop on the pathway and look down at her.

"What?"

She shook her head. "I notice that when you talk about your grandmother, you lose your accent."

He smiled. "It has its benefits," he said, speaking in a French accent.

"I bet. How many women fall for that old trick?"

He shrugged, wrapping his arm around her shoulders. "Enough."

"Do you see your parents often?" she asked as they made their way towards the pool deck.

"Every year. Either I go to them or they come to us."

"What do they think of your career choice?" she asked as they made their way back to the employees' apartment building.

"My father is appalled. My mother, however, couldn't care less as long as it doesn't interfere with her social life."

He held open the door for her and she felt a spike of nerves rush through her. They walked up the stairs in silence. She stopped just outside her doorway.

"Goodnight, Lilly." It came out as a whisper.

"Aren't you…" He placed a finger over her lips, then dipped his head down and replaced it with his lips.

"Soon. When the time is right." He kissed her again, causing her knees to turn to jelly. Her fingers rushed through his hair, holding him to her, wanting the moment to last forever.

Then, too soon, he took a step back. "I'll wait until you go in and make sure everything is in its place."

She smiled. "I started locking my door again."

"Wise choice."

"It's a shame, I've lived here for years and always felt safe. Until now."

"We'll work on finding out who broke in, tomorrow."

She nodded, then sighed. "If we make it through the Robinson clan."

He smiled. "Thank you for handling it tonight."

"It's my job," she added, then she stepped into her

room. Everything looked in place, so she turned back to him. "Goodnight."

"Night, Lilly." He leaned in and placed a soft kiss on her lips.

When she shut the door behind her, she closed her eyes and replayed how her nickname sounded coming from his lips.

She showered and changed, and then her cell phone buzzed with a message from Sarah.

-How did it go? BTW, I hate that you turned off your ringer.

-We survived. Sorry, it got busy. Forgive your BFF?

-Always! Love ya. TTY tomorrow?

-Yup, night.

She set her phone on her nightstand and pulled her covers back to climb in, only to see a green piece of paper tucked under her pillow.

Frowning, she pulled it out and stared at it for a moment before unfolding it.

Are you trying to make me jealous? STOP!

Her eyes moved over to her door. She was sure she had locked it. Playing over the last few minutes in her head, she remembered pulling her keys out and unlocking the door.

Then how did someone get into her room and leave this note? She felt a shiver run down her spine. Had it been here since the night of the break-in?

The first night she'd slept in Heather's room, so she wouldn't have noticed it. The next night, she'd spent half the night playing dress up for Adam, then had fallen into bed outside of the blankets and had only gotten a few hours of restless sleep. She doubted she would have noticed a boulder hiding under her pillow, let alone a small piece of paper.

Deciding to show Adam the following day as a clue to the break-in, she tucked the note in her nightstand and quickly changed the sheets of her bed. She tossed the old sheets into her trash bin. Still, instead of crawling under the blankets, she pulled a new blanket from her closet and wrapped herself in it then crawled into the oversized chair in the corner and stared at her bed.

By the next morning, her eyes burned, her head ached, and she had decided to see about getting a new mattress.

Morning shifts were Adam's favorite time of day. He enjoyed waking up early and seeing the sunrise, smelling the fresh-brewed coffee and the warm bread baking in the oven, and knowing he was the only one who enjoyed being awake that early.

His crew of eight was present for every meal during the day. They rotated shifts, two weeks on the island, two weeks off. It made most of the staff happier.

He, however, worked three weeks on, four days off, which suited him best. He knew he was set to go off shift early Monday morning after the big group left, but he wanted to hang around and spend more time with Lilly, since she was working straight through with no breaks until Sarah and Ben returned. He'd planned on talking to her about it when he saw her later that day.

Things usually ran smoothly for breakfast, since it was the easiest menu they had. However, that morning, two of his staff had complained about stomach issues, and he had sent them back to their rooms. Now, short staffed, he found himself rushing around the kitchen like it was his first day on the job.

Pans went unwashed, food sat in the heater for longer than it should have, and someone had actually written an order down wrong. He was pissed.

After the rush, he retreated into his office and called for backup. Rachelle, his other line cook, who subbed for Tara, was available and agreed to be there before the lunch rush. Rob was not available to fill in for Steven, however, so they were still down one person. Lunch and dinner were going to be rough.

They made it through lunch without a hitch, and he realized he had yet to see Lilly that day. Normally she came into the kitchen during her break for lunch, but today, she had requested that her food be brought up to Sarah's office. He had been too busy to run it up himself.

If she didn't show up in the kitchen by dinner, he was determined to hunt her down. He knew the party for the Robinson clan was happening upstairs since the kitchen was a zoo. Thankfully, this time, no plates were returned and as far as he knew, the party went off without a hitch. He imagined Lilly had been so busy upstairs that she hadn't had time to eat.

Less than half an hour after dinner shift, the kitchen phone rang, and he overheard Rachelle take Lilly's order.

"I'll take it up myself," he told Rachelle. He made sure everything on the tray was perfect before climbing the stairs.

He knocked on the door and walked in to see a man holding Lilly to the desk, his mouth inches from hers. Her fists were balled, and she held them between her and the man. But it was the fear in her eyes that made Adam drop the tray and rush across the room.

Before he knew it, he had the man pinned against the wall.

"Adam don't hurt him," Lilly said somewhere behind him. His mind registered her words and reminded him that this might be a guest, but the irrational part of his mind wanted to smash the man's face in.

"Did he hurt you?" he asked, not taking his eyes off the guy, who was clearly too drunk to care what was going on.

"No, we just had a slight misunderstanding," she said, walking over and putting her hand on his arm. "Please, let Mr. Robinson go."

Hearing the name snapped him to attention and his arms dropped away, causing the man to stumble slightly.

"Sorry about this," Lilly said to the guest, causing Adam's jaw to tense.

The man had looked like he was attacking Lilly, and she was the one apologizing!

Adam stood back and watched her walk over to her door, then waited until the guest walked out, giving him a backward glance as he left.

"Why did you do that?" she asked when they were finally alone.

"Why?" He almost choked on the word. "Why did *you* do *that*?" He turned it on her. "Why apologize for the jerk pinning you down and almost molesting you?"

"That isn't..." She sighed and rubbed her hands on the side of her head. For the first time since he'd walked into the room, he noticed how tired she looked. Her eyes were bloodshot, and her face was paler than he liked.

"What's wrong? Are you sick?" He moved over to her,

taking her shoulders into his hands so he could have a better look at her.

"No," she started to say, then he felt her slump against him and quickly pulled her into his arms as she sighed into his chest. "I'm okay, really," she said into his shirt.

"If he upset you that bad..."

"No, it wasn't him," she said as she leaned back slightly.

"Lilly, I can't help you if you don't talk to me," he added after a moment of silence.

She closed her eyes and leaned back against the desk. "Let's just say that I can't wait until Sarah gets back."

"Are things that bad around here?" He glanced over her shoulder at the desk. There were several piles of paperwork, and the computer was flashing the blue screen of death.

"No, but with everything else..." She sighed, then pointed to the computer. "I had just entered all of that"— she nodded to the large stack of bills— "into the system when that happened. Then Tristen walked in." She started to walk behind the desk, but he stopped her.

"Why don't you take a quick break, eat something." He groaned and looked down at the mess that used to be her perfect meal. "Sorry." He frowned as he walked over to see if he could salvage any of it. When he removed the lid to the tray, he groaned again. The noodles were everywhere on the platter, the sauce looked like it had exploded everywhere, even in the vegetables.

"It's fine," she said, kneeling next to him. "It looks and smells wonderful."

"It's a mess. I'll head down and get you another..."

"No," She laid her hand on his arm again. "Really, it's

okay." She picked up the tray herself and carried it to the desk. She flipped off the computer and waited until it booted up again.

He walked over and sat in a chair across from her then watched her take her first forkful of his angel hair chicken pasta.

"Mmm." Her eyes closed as she enjoyed the first bite.

"It's normally a lot prettier..."

Her eyes opened, stopping him. "Looks aren't everything." Her eyes darted to the door and he understood that she was talking about her unwanted visitor from earlier.

"No, I suppose they aren't." He smiled.

CHAPTER 8

*L*ilith was thankful Adam had walked in when he had. She had just been winding herself up to clock Tristen when her door opened. She was pretty sure she could have gotten out of his grip, but a sense of relief had washed over her when Adam stormed in.

Over the years, she'd had plenty of unwanted attention, which she had dealt with quickly, herself. But no one had ever hunted her down after what she could only assume was an entire bottle of Jameson from the bar. Which reminded her that she needed to talk to Scott, the bartender on duty, about their policy of cutting a patron off. Tristen should have never been allowed to drink as much as he had.

"So, how bad is it?" Adam asked, breaking into her thoughts.

"What?" She'd forgotten she was retyping all the numbers into the accounting software.

"That." He nodded to the pile.

"Oh, not bad. Just an hour of work I have to redo."

"Don't you save often?" he asked, prompting her to glare at him.

"Of course, I do." She bit her tongue and refused to admit that she'd forgotten to earlier. Hitting the save button now, she smiled at him and scooped up another bite of noodles. "Don't you have dishes to do?"

He laughed and leaned back in the chair, then shocked her by putting his feet up on the edge of the desk and crossing his arms behind his head. "Nope, the staff can handle cleanup. They're probably already done by now."

She frowned over at him, then went back to work.

"What is all that anyway?" He nodded to the pile.

"Bills," she said without looking up.

"I know that, but why are you putting them in manually?"

"Because it's how Sarah does it." She started on the next invoice.

"Why not scan them in?"

"Because this is how Sarah does it."

He shook his head, moved behind her, and took the mouse from her.

"Stop." She swatted his hand away, but he just smiled down at her.

"Move over." He nudged her until the chair was pushed aside. He leaned over the computer. "I thought so," he said under his breath. "Here." He clicked a few buttons, then took the stack of invoices, tapped them until they all lay in a nice pile, walked over to her scanner, and set them on the top tray. When they started being pulled in, piece by piece, she frowned at the screen as each invoice automatically entered itself into the software.

"How'd…" She frowned and glanced over at him. "How did you do that?"

He leaned back against the large scanner and chuckled. "I used the same system at my last job."

"You just saved me… hours," she added, feeling conflicted. "All week long I've dreaded this job."

"Well, now you don't have to."

"Why doesn't Sarah know about this?" She added a new pile of bills to the scanner and watched the screen as everything was inputted.

"It even adds them to the right category." She shook her head in disbelief.

"Accounting for Dummies," he said, running a finger down her arm.

She turned to him. "Are you calling me a dummy?" She watched his face turn to horror.

"No!" He dropped his hands, then took her shoulders. "I didn't mean…"

She smiled at him. "I know. I was just teasing." She watched his face turn again. "You're so easy to rile up."

He pulled her closer until she felt her breath hitch. This his lips covered hers and her knees turned to jelly. If he hadn't been holding onto her, she would have slid to the floor.

"I could say the same about you." His hands roamed slowly over her back, sending waves of goosebumps throughout her entire body.

"You're not playing fair," she said, her voice a little breathless.

"Neither are you. You've been hiding from me all day." When he saw the truth in her eyes, he frowned. "Why?"

She pulled back slightly and shook her head. "No reason." His eyebrows shot up and she sighed. "I guess I didn't want the distraction. I had a lot to do this morning."

"I could have helped."

"What kind of boss would I be if I allowed you to stop your work to help me?"

"First"—he held up his finger— "you're not my boss." She smiled at that. "Second, I have enough employees to help…" She raised her eyebrows and tilted her head. "Well, okay, today I was short… for breakfast," he added quickly.

"Adam, I was just busy, not swamped. Besides, you just saved me from sitting here the rest of the evening." She removed the last stack from the scanner and shoved all the invoices into the done folder. "There." She dusted her hands off and then turned to him. "I heard you had chocolate truffle cake tonight. Any chance that you have any left over?"

He smiled. "How about we head down and see, then take it out to the beach and enjoy it under the stars?"

"Sounds good to me." She locked up the office on their way out. "Oh, I have something I want you to look at." She took his hand and instead of heading down the front grand staircase, took him around back to the employee staircase, then out the back door towards the employees' quarters building. He remained silent as they climbed up the stairs towards their floor.

"What is it?" he finally asked when they were on their floor.

"Something I found last night." She unlocked her door and hesitated at the opening. Reaching in, she flipped on her light and quickly scanned the empty room. Taking a deep breath, she entered and rushed over to her nightstand. When she opened the drawer, she gasped.

The green piece of paper was nowhere to be found. Pulling out the drawer completely, she dumped its contents onto the unmade bed.

"Where is it?" She searched, then when she didn't find it, did the same to the bottom drawer. "It was here last night." She got onto her hands and knees and looked under her bed and around the nightstand and even walked over to her desk to look through the drawers there.

"Lilly, what was it?"

"A note." She turned to him. "On a green piece of paper." She turned back towards her newly replenished closet and debated tossing all the clothes out onto the bed once more.

"Hey." His hands on her shoulders stopped her. "I'm sure it's here. Your door was locked and before you dumped everything out, it didn't look like anyone had been in here."

"Yes, I suppose you're right." She bit her bottom lip. "I..." She sighed. "I could have taken it with me this morning and left it in Sarah's office. I was very tired." She rolled her shoulders.

"We can swing through the kitchen first, then head back upstairs to check." She nodded, her eyes still darting around the room as she tried to remember if she'd taken it with her. He rubbed her arms. "I'm sure you will find it. What did the note say anyway?"

"Are you trying to make me jealous? STOP!"

He frowned at her. "What does that mean?"

She shrugged her shoulders. "I'm not sure. For a moment, I thought..." She dropped off. She walked over to the door and waited until he followed her out. She made sure to lock her door once more behind her.

Adam surprised her by reaching down and tugging on her locked door. When it popped open, she gasped. "How did you…"

He leaned down and examined her door handle. She watched him pull a piece of tape from the door jam. She leaned against the wall and felt her head spin.

"Easy." His voice was right beside her. "Breathe."

"Someone…" She took a deep breath. "Someone's been coming in. Even after…"

"Lilly." Adam's voice was so smooth. Just hearing the nickname made her heart settle slightly. "Let's head downstairs." He took her hand and she followed him until the cool night air hit her. She stopped just outside the door and took several deep breaths.

Her mind was whirling over what they had just discovered. Her knees buckled as she thought of the possibility that someone had snuck in while she'd been asleep, or when she'd been in the shower.

"Hey." Adam took her shoulders and pulled her towards a bench where most of the employees who smoked went at night. "What's gotten into you?" he asked as he shoved her head between her knees.

"Someone…" She felt her body jerk and she shut her eyes as tears poured out. Then a terrible thought hit her. "Someone was in my room last night while I was there."

"What?" He sat up, his entire body on guard. "How do you know?"

"I don't, but the note." Her voice was muffled since she was still leaning down. "It's gone."

He relaxed back. "You said yourself that you could have taken it to Sarah's office this morning."

"I didn't," she said, sitting back up and then resting her head back. Tears slid down her face and she wiped them away.

"We can still check," he suggested. She glanced over at him, then nodded. He held out his hand and helped her stand and then immediately pulled her into a hug. "Why don't you crash in my room for a few nights?"

She laughed. "Is that the best pick-up line you've got?"

He pulled back slightly and smiled. "I've got others, but the fact is, I'll be gone for four nights starting Monday."

She thought about it. "What about until then?"

"I'll sleep on my sofa." The thing was half his size, but he'd sleep much better knowing she was safe and he could watch over her.

"I couldn't… I can stay with Heather."

"Well, I had an idea about that." His mind quickly worked out a plan. "Let's get some dessert and take a walk to work things out."

She nodded and took his hand. He not only packed them the truffle cake but added a bottle of wine to one of the picnic baskets they used for guests who wanted to have a picnic lunch.

Instead of heading to the beach, he pulled her down the pathway that circled the island, then doubled back towards the small cottage that only employees and some very intuitive guests knew about.

"Why here?" Lilly asked when he unlocked the door with the master key he had.

"We need to make sure no one listens in on what I have planned."

She paused at the door and glared at him. "What?"

He chuckled and tugged on her hand until she walked into the small cottage. The place was the size of a shed but was straight out of a fairy tale. Most guests actually mistook it for a shed, if they ever stumbled across it.

It was nestled back in thick bushes and trees along a pathway few ever took.

"Trust me. I have a few ideas on how to trap whoever is breaking into your room."

He saw her shiver and glance over her shoulder into the darkness. "You... you don't think they followed..."

"No, that's why I took the other pathway. I wanted to make sure we were alone." He shut the door behind him after listening for any sounds outside. "I think it worked. Besides, this place has thick walls. I don't think anyone can listen in."

"So?" She walked over and sat at the small kitchen booth area. "What's this great plan of yours?" She crossed her arms over her chest and he could tell she felt nervous.

He set the basket down on the table and took his time getting them each a slice of cake and a glass of wine.

"Well, for starters, you're going to be spending your nights in my room. With me." He watched her as he took a drink of his wine.

She stopped and stared at him. "Oh," she said when it dawned on her. "Are you trying to make me jealous?"

He nodded quickly. "At least that's what I'm thinking."

"Okay, so we set him—and at this point, we can assume it's him—off?"

"Yes. Then, on Monday, we'll make a show of me leaving, heading into town for my scheduled days off."

"But?" she asked, taking a bite of the cake.

"But, I'll double back, take my small boat back to the island."

"You have a boat?"

"Yes, a small one. In case I need to come back for emergencies." She nodded.

"Okay, then what?"

"You continue to stay in my room, instead of in yours. But, you act like you're sleeping in your room, where I will be instead."

"We," she interjected.

"No," he said, finishing off his cake. "I."

She leaned back, crossed her arms over her chest again. This time it was in defiance instead of nerves.

"No, we will stay in my room. Besides, if he sees me sneaking into your room..."

Damn it, she was right. If whoever was watching saw her go into his room... a million thoughts jumped into his mind and fear had him reaching for his empty wine glass.

Pouring some more for them both, he nodded. "Okay, we will be in your room, waiting for him."

"Then what?" she asked, taking a sip of wine.

"Then..." He shrugged. "I will detain him until the police arrive."

"You make that part sound so easy."

"It is," he added, sure of himself.

"What if he has a weapon?"

"Cowards like this never do," he supplied, causing her to laugh.

"I suppose you've dealt with a lot of situations like this before." She pushed her empty plate aside.

"Well, not exactly. I did catch one of my employees at my last job stealing from the cash register. I set things up to make everyone believe I had left for the evening…" He sighed and shrugged. "You get the rest."

"And it worked?"

He nodded. "Like a charm." He reached over and took her hand. He could tell she'd gone back to worrying. "Whoever is breaking in and doing this… we'll catch him. I don't like seeing you look like you didn't get any sleep." He rubbed his thumb down her cheek, over the dark circles under her eyes.

"I'm fine…" His finger moved down to cover her lips.

"I can see you're not." He pulled her close. "You've been jumping at shadows, sleeping in your chair instead of in your bed." When she tensed and looked at him, he chuckled. "It was obvious since your sheets were in the trash and your bed was empty. Besides the red eyes and bags here." He touched her face lightly, then leaned down and placed a feather-light kiss where his fingers had just been.

"Adam?" she said between kisses. Somehow, he'd gone from soft kisses to deeper, more passionate ones without knowing. Pulling back quickly, he moved to stand up, but she held him in place.

"I'm sorry." He shook his head. "I should have…"

"Finished what you started?" she supplied, pushing her hands into his hair and holding him to her lips once more.

"Lilly… you… deserve more," he said between her lips brushing over his.

"Then give me more," she said against his skin and he knew they were not going to make it back to his room for the night.

CHAPTER 9

She tried not to shiver when Adam lifted her up into his arms gently. His mouth was so soft against her skin, showing her tenderness the likes of which she'd never experienced before.

The cabin was so small, when he carried her up the narrow staircase to the loft, she had to duck. He laid her down on the oversized mattress that took up the entire space, then just looked down at her. He was on his knees, and she reached up to pull him towards her.

"I've thought about this," he said in a low tone as he looked at her, his eyes roaming over her face. "I've imagined it a thousand times."

"Me too." She loved the feel of his hair under her fingertips. The softness of it in her hands. When his lips touched hers again, she wished more than anything that she could hold onto this moment forever.

Her hands roamed down his neck to his shoulders and a slight moan escaped when she felt them bunch under her fingertips. When his hands moved, they pulled her shirt higher until she felt his fingers brush her naked skin underneath.

She couldn't stop the moan from escaping her lips, or the need from building inside her. Her legs wrapped around his hips, holding him closer to her body as she felt something she'd never imagined before. Her entire body vibrated as his hands moved slowly over her.

"Easy," he said against her skin. Then his mouth left hers and traveled down her neck until he found the spot just above her collarbone. She felt him shift and closed her eyes when his hardness pressed against her core.

"Please," she begged, not knowing if she could wait much longer.

"I'm enjoying myself too much to hurry." He chuckled against her skin. He'd worked on her shirt buttons and before she knew it, she was exposed to his view. He leaned up and gently pulled the silk from her shoulders.

"Beautiful," he whispered before his head dipped down to cover her exposed breast. He tugged on the strap of her bra, sending it down until that too was removed.

His eyes slowly moved over every inch of her exposed skin and she saw them heat. Then his lips heated her skin as he trailed kisses over the same pathway.

Her fingers dug into his shoulders as she felt herself building, her hips jerked against his. Demanding. Wanting. Needing.

She reached for his shirt, then waited when he leaned back to pull it over his head. His chest was even more impressive than she'd imagined. Her hands reached out and she trailed her fingers over his bare skin.

"Lilly," he moaned. "I wanted to go slow, but you're driving me crazy." He chuckled.

"Good, now you know how I feel." She started to reach for his jeans, but he pulled back and shook his head.

"No, not that fast." He smiled. "Let me…" With his fingertip, he inched her pencil skirt up until it was almost to the top of her thighs. "I want to take care of you first."

Just having his hands touch her where she'd never allowed another to go had her hips jerking underneath him. His fingers swept softly to her inner thigh, causing her eyes to close in pure pleasure.

"You're so soft," she heard him say. She was shocked when he dipped a finger underneath her silk panties. Her shoulders bounded off the bed when he touched her. Then his finger sank inside her slowly and she fell back onto the bed as he played with her softness.

"Adam," she begged, tossing her head from side to side. She didn't know what was building inside, only that soon, she felt she would explode into nothingness.

"Soon," he said, then she felt him slide her panties down her legs until he rested between her knees. When she felt his wet tongue against her inner thigh, she tensed.

"Easy," he murmured. "You taste like heaven." He trailed kisses along the inside of her thigh until she relaxed back against the bed.

His hot mouth trailed higher and she tensed once more until his mouth covered her. Then she did explode, crying out his name as her fingers dug into his hair, holding him, begging him for more.

She'd never experienced anything like it before. Her entire body shuddered and jerked until she felt him pin her down to the bed with his weight as he settled between her legs. Only then did she realize that he was completely naked.

"Adam?" She started to tense, but his hands moved in slow, small circles, relaxing her once more.

"I've got you," he said next to her lips.

"Yes." She closed her eyes and turned herself over to the feeling of him sliding slowly into her.

Sex had never been something she'd desired, nor something she'd ever imagined she would enjoy. Her body easily relaxed around his, taking him in until she felt every touch, every soft caress.

She knew that it wouldn't last, that soon her body would convulse again, but her mind kept screaming for her to hold out. Just one more moment.

His mouth covered hers. Her fingers dug into his hips as he moved over her, in her, thrusting deeper, longer than she could have dreamed.

A moment before she felt her own release, Adam tensed over her and she allowed herself to follow him.

He must have slept for a while. The soft breathing next to his skin and the tingle of Lilly's hair on his chest woke him almost an hour before the sun normally did.

He glanced down at her and smiled. She was fast asleep in his arms, her leg tucked over his and her hand sprawled on his chest. He could stay like this forever, but his inner clock told him that it was time to start the morning shift. The guests would be waking up soon. Today would be an easier day than yesterday since the large group was leaving before lunchtime. The next group of guests would be arriving just before dinner.

Hopefully, he could persuade Lilly to have another picnic lunch with him down on the beach.

Then he heard the thunder outside and groaned.

"What?" she said against his skin.

"It's raining." He tried to get a glance out the window, but he'd shut the blinds when they had arrived.

"Yes, it's supposed to rain until Tuesday, then again later next week."

He groaned. "I was hoping to persuade you to go with me on a picnic for lunch."

"And?" She leaned up and looked down at him, her hair falling over her shoulders.

"And, since it's raining—" Thunder crashed again. "And pretty good, from the sounds of it, I guess we'll have to settle for eating—"

"In the pavilion?" she suggested.

"Not if there's lightning that goes along with all that thunder. How about…" He thought about it. "How about the attic?"

She frowned. "The attic? Which one?"

"The one in the main building. I went up there once when I got turned around, shortly after I started working here. Anyway, it's pretty large and there's some really cool furniture up there. We can make ourselves at home and find a place to finish plotting out our trap."

He sat up slightly, taking her with him. Just the feel of her skin against his had his body reacting.

"Sounds good." She moaned and started to stretch over him, but he was quick and pulled her atop him instead.

"But first." His mouth took hers as he slid once more into her heat. "Breakfast."

Less than an hour later, Adam walked into the kitchen

whistling. Even the poor weather outside couldn't dampen his mood.

He seemed to spread his good mood to everyone, and breakfast whizzed by. After the kitchen died down, he poured everything he had into making their picnic lunch a perfect meal.

Since they couldn't have perfect weather, he decided to make perfect-weather food. He started with a creamy summer pasta salad, then added some German potato salad, along with orecchiette with pesto and oven-roasted tomatoes. Then he made crispy sweet potatoes, and for the main dish, lobster rolls with lemon herb butter. Rachelle's specialty chocolate chip s'mores would be the perfect end to a summer's meal.

He grabbed a bottle of Lilly's favorite wine and packed everything into a large basket. He headed up half an hour early to make sure everything was perfect before she arrived.

He found the attic exactly as he remembered it, dusty and full of old-time charm. There were several large pieces of furniture pushed up against a wall and covered with sheets.

He flipped the white sheets up and found an antique thirty-inch round pedestal table with two bentwood chairs, a set his grandmother would be envious of. He pulled out the white tablecloth and started setting the table.

After the table was perfect, he continued his search and found several paintings and set them up around the table for atmosphere. He pulled a few boxes down, so that the lighting would be better then switched off the neon overheads. Lighting the silver-plated candelabra, he had found under a pile of books, he sat back and surveyed his masterpiece.

Music! He rushed around the room looking for the old radio he'd seen up here earlier. Finally finding it, he pulled it over to a plug and prayed that it still worked. When the light came on and static echoed in the room, he twisted the dial until he found a station that played soft music, then he turned the volume low.

"Wow," Lilly said from behind him. He turned around and lost his breath. She'd changed from the pencil skirt and silk blouse she'd worn last night into a flowing cream-colored summer dress that hugged her curves. Curves he enjoyed very much.

"Yes, wow." He walked towards her and took her hand as his eyes moved slowly over her.

"This looks amazing." She nodded to the table. "I didn't know all of this stuff was up here."

"I think no one else does as well." He leaned down and placed a kiss gently on her lips, then took her hand and walked her towards the table in the middle of the room.

"I always loved that window." She nodded to the massive floor-to-ceiling arched window. The unique shape of it was part of the charm that East Haven's main building held. Its shape mimicked the windows on the main floor and the arches in the main entrance and hallways. "This is bigger than I remember." She glanced around as she sat down.

"You've been up here before?"

"Yes, but it was so packed with boxes"—she glanced towards the window again— "there wasn't much to see."

He sat across from her and poured them both some wine. When he lifted the lids to the food, her eyes lit up.

"Wow, it's like a real picnic." She smiled. "It smells so good." She leaned in and closed her eyes as she took a deep breath.

He watched her eat, but when she stopped and glanced up at him, he realized he hadn't touched his food yet.

"So, when do we start setting the trap?" she asked as she took a sip of her wine.

"Tonight. If it's alright with you." He glanced up. "I'd like to start spreading the word that we are… involved." He held his breath.

She frowned slightly, and he wondered if she knew how rapidly his heart was beating.

"What do you think that will do?" She bit her bottom lip and set down her fork. She shook her head, and her hair fell around her shoulders. She'd worn it down today, and he liked the look very much.

"For starters, I think whoever left the note will be forced to do something unexpected. Which, if you've ever watched a good detective show, always proves beneficial in catching the perp."

She giggled. "Okay, so we force him to be sloppy."

He nodded and smiled. "If all of this is about you"— his smile fell away— "about his feelings for you, then the knowledge that we're an item will piss him off."

"But"—she leaned closer— "why wreck my room? Why trash my stuff in the first place? Why not just leave the note?"

He shrugged. "Maybe he's confused."

"Speaking of confusion, I've got a list." She leaned up and pulled a folded piece of paper from the pocket of her sundress. "Of employees I think would fit the profile."

His smile returned. "So do I." He pulled out his list from his back pocket and handed it to her.

For the next half an hour they glanced over the lists, debating the names. Some they crossed off. In the end, they had a list of ten people, all of the employees he had never liked. If it was up to him, several of them would be literally off the island.

"So, what's the next step?" she asked finishing the last bite of her food.

Leaning down, he pulled out the box of dessert, set it between them, and opened it. "The next step is; we show everyone on the island that we're together."

Her eyes were glued to the s'mores. "How do we do that?"

He handed her a plate with the dessert on it. "Well, I figured after we finish this meal, we head down where we can"—his eyes locked with hers— "make a public display of ourselves."

Her lips curved up. "Now that sounds fun." She took a bite of the s'more and moaned with pleasure.

"If you keep moaning like that, we might have a private showing first." Her cheeks flushed and he decided he enjoyed making her blush.

Lilly helped with the cleanup, then glanced around the room once more. "You know; this would make a great ballroom."

He looked around again. "What would we need a ballroom for?"

"Weddings, parties, events…" She tilted her head. "A row of chairs along that wall, a glass bar there." She pointed and spun around, then glanced down. "The flooring would need to be sanded and stained, but other than that…" She broke off. "I bet it wouldn't take more than a few thousand dollars to fix it up."

"Where would all this stuff go?" He motioned to the boxes and furniture.

"Some of it, like the table and chairs, would stay. Pushed up against a wall or over there in the corner." She walked around and looked behind some boxes. "There's more back here too."

He nodded, then walked over to look. "Yes, some cabinets and I think some clocks and odd pieces in some of the boxes." She turned and looked at him. "I was looking for candle holders." He took her hand and pulled her to the other side of the room. "There's a sofa back here that looks like a Louis XV." He moved a few boxes and exposed the red velvet sofa.

Lilly gasped. "I can't believe all of this is just hidden up here." She smiled at him. "I'm beginning to think we found the best welcome home present for Sarah and Ben."

He looked at her, not understanding.

"This." She motioned around. "All of this. Cleaning this up, setting it up."

He laughed. "How do you expect we get all this done in…"—he glanced at his watch sarcastically— "less than a week?

She smiled. "I have my ways." She walked over and took up the picnic basket and waited for him at the door. "Trust me."

He shrugged his shoulders, took the basket from her, then took her hand in his and walked down the hallway to show everyone on the island exactly how he felt about her.

CHAPTER 10

$\mathcal{L}$ilith had never imagined that Adam's idea of showing everyone they were together was pushing her up against the wall and making every bone in her body melt while lighting every inch of her skin on fire. His mouth and hands had a way of making her forget time and place.

She hadn't even heard or noticed anyone else in the room. But when he pulled back, the silence of the kitchen was almost deafening. He leaned close and, smiling, said, "I think that should do it. Don't you?"

She was still a little fuzzy and instead of answering, just nodded.

"I'll see you after dinner?" he asked, rubbing a finger over her lips slowly.

Again, she nodded.

"Good. I'll try to bring you up dinner. You can supply the dessert this time." He leaned in and placed a soft kiss on her lips, then nudged her towards the door.

She walked out without a word. It wasn't until she

entered the main dining room that she remembered to breathe.

"There you are." Tristen rushed across the room towards her and she felt her entire body go on guard. When his hand reached out, she flinched slightly. It wasn't as if she was afraid of the man, it was just that her mind was still reeling from Adam. Instantly, Tristen dropped his hand. "I…" He glanced around, then dropped his voice. "I had hoped that I would see you before we left. I wanted to apologize for yesterday."

"No need," she said, not sure why she instantly felt like she needed to comfort him.

"Yes, yes, there is. I…" He sighed. "Kaleen can be a bitch." He glanced around the room quickly, no doubt making sure the woman wasn't within earshot. "I'm only with her because our parents are friends." He slowly reached out and took her arm and then led them towards the patio doors. She followed him, knowing they would remain in view of the entire dining room.

"I hope your stay was…" She started her standard speech.

"I'd like to see you again," he broke in.

She swayed back and blinked up at him a few times. "I… I'm flattered."

"Just flattered?" he asked.

"I… I'm seeing someone," she blurted out.

"The Frenchman?" he asked after a moment.

"Yes."

His eyes moved to the kitchen doors. "Lucky man," he said, then turned back towards her. "Well, I hope there are no hard feelings. I really am sorry."

Just then her phone rang. Glancing down, she sighed.

"I'm sorry, I have to…" He nodded, and she stepped out onto the patio to answer the call from Sarah.

Before she even got the words "hello" out, Sarah was talking.

"What is this I hear about you and Adam?" she demanded.

"Um." She calculated that it had been less than five minutes since their kiss in the kitchen. There was no way Sarah could have heard about it yet. "What have you heard?" she asked, walking over to the railing of the porch and looking out at the rain.

"That you two caught a wine thief."

Lilith's shoulders relaxed. "Oh, that."

"Oh, that?" Sarah sounded hurt. "Is there more that I don't know about?"

Lilith closed her eyes. "Um." She took a deep breath and spent the next ten minutes catching her friend up on everything that had happened.

By the time she was done, it felt like an enormous weight had been lifted from her shoulders. She even had to wipe away a tear or two when Sarah asked why she'd felt she needed to hide all of this from her.

"Because you're on your freaking honeymoon!" She sighed. "You're not supposed to worry about this kind of stuff."

"I don't worry. I left East Haven in capable hands," Sarah added, making Lilith feel even worse for keeping it from her. "Besides, I remember telling you to let me know the moment Adam finally made his move on you."

"Finally?" She turned and leaned against the railing, glancing into the front door where the entire Robinson clan was standing around with their luggage. They had all crowded into their private yachts to get here, but since the weather had taken a turn for the worse, it appeared that no one was willing to brave the rain to leave. She could see Tristen in the mix. It appeared that he was arguing with the brunette beauty.

While she was watching, he turned towards the window and waved for her to come in. She could tell there was an issue and dreaded what was going to come next.

"I can't get into this right now." She broke in as Sarah was asking question after question about what had happened between her and Adam. "There seems to be an issue with the Robinsons I need to go handle."

"Oh, okay, but call me later. And Lilith, don't leave me in the dark again. We're sisters, even if not by blood."

Lilith closed her eyes when they stung with emotion. "I'll call you later." Her mind flashed to how she wanted to spend her evening with Adam. "Actually, make it in the morning. I'm… we're setting our trap tonight."

"Right." Her friend dragged the word out. "Just make sure you're… very careful and… protected…"

Lilith chuckled, then gasped. They hadn't used protection last night. Nor had she ever thought about birth control.

"Lilith?"

"I… have to go." She hung up without another word and then forced her mind to focus on solving the problem inside.

Later, she told herself. She would deal with all that later. She was determined to not make that mistake again. There were plenty of condoms in the employees' store. She would make sure she swung by the place before heading up to bed with Adam.

When she walked in, she was bombarded with the noise of unhappy guests. Walking over to the main desk, she moved behind it and leaned towards Stacey, who looked completely flustered.

"I'm sorry, Miss Brown. It appears that the entire Robinson group would like to extend their stay until the weather lets up."

Her eyebrows shot up, but she quickly recovered, then punched a few keys on the computer and gauged how she could make it work. Then she turned to the group.

"I think we could make this work," she started and was surprised when the room grew silent. "However, we will need to have a few of you bunk up together." The noise started, but she continued to talk. "I'm not talking about putting strangers in with you, only immediate family members. Kids in with parents, brothers, and sisters in the same suite." She waited as everyone discussed their options. "Of course I'd be willing to discount the rooms until Wednesday. That's when we're supposed to get a break in the weather."

Again, she waited, then everyone nodded in agreement. "Very well. Stacey, I've already put them into the system, all you have to do is get them checked in again." She leaned in. "Give them a ten percent discount on the rooms only. Oh, and have Joe find someplace to store all their luggage until the rooms have been turned over."

"Yes, ma'am." She smiled and looked relieved.

"Thank you for being patient. Stacey is going to take good care of you." She started to walk away, but her arm was grabbed. Turning, she held her smile for Tristen.

"Thanks for handling that. Um, I wanted to make sure…" He glanced over towards Kaleen.

"She's in with her parents, so are you," she added, touching his arm lightly.

"Thanks." He took a step back and disappeared into the crowd. She made her way up the stairs and decided she would take care of the new stack of invoices for the day.

She walked into the office, leaned against the door, and played over everything that had happened in the last few hours. No doubt by now the entire island knew about her and Adam. She wondered how long they would have to wait for whoever had broken into her room to make his first move. She felt a jolt of excitement rush through her. Somehow, Adam made it all seem like a game.

Walking over, she picked up the stack of invoices, tapped them until they fell in line, and then almost screamed when a small green piece of paper fell from them.

She felt her knees go weak and slid into the seat as her eyes zeroed in on the bold lettering.

"Stop messing with him! You're mine! Forever!"

She reached for the phone but stopped herself when she noticed how badly her hand was shaking.

"What do you mean they're staying on?" Adam growled out, causing Mat, one of his staff to take a step back.

"I… Miss Brown… she arranged it. The entire group is staying until Wednesday."

Adam felt his blood begin to boil. Setting down a pan he'd been holding, he stormed from the kitchen and up the back stairs and didn't even bother to knock on the office door.

"Why the hell didn't you tell me that the group of fifty people was staying on for three more nights!" He leaned his fists against the desk.

Her head had snapped up, and she frowned at him. "I…" She blinked, and he realized she looked like she was going to pass out.

"What's wrong?" He moved towards her quickly.

"There's another note." She pointed down to the ground.

He walked around and stood there, looking down at the bold print.

"Stop messing with him! You're mine! Forever!"

"Where was it?" He moved to pick it up from the ground.

"In..." She took a deep breath. "In the invoices there." She pointed to the stack sitting on the edge of the desk.

Then she blinked and groaned. "Damn it, I knew I forgot something."

"What?" He almost jumped back.

"The Robinsons. I forgot to tell you they were staying on."

"Don't worry about them."

"But that's fifty more mouths to feed and I just called your order for the next week. Now I'll have to go and…"

He took her shoulders and forced her to stand up and look at him.

"I forgot," she said in a low voice. "You can easily call and correct your order."

His eyes scanned her. "It's okay. You've been crying?"

Her shoulders relaxed. "Wouldn't you? This means they broke in here, too."

"At least now we have the note." He tucked it into his

pocket and decided to do some detective work himself. "Are you okay?" He ran his hands up and down her arms and noticed they were chilled.

"I had a call from Sarah," she informed him, glancing around the room.

"Is she okay?" he asked, trying to take her mind off of the note.

"Yes, I just... told her... everything." She bit her lip and he could see the worry in her eyes.

"And?" She was silent, and he added, "Did she unfriend you?"

Lilly chuckled, and he could see her eyes clear. "No, of course not."

"So, then what's the problem?"

"I feel like I disappointed her." Her eyes darted down to where the note had been moments ago.

"By?" He took her hands and pulled her closer since it felt like the conversation wasn't going far enough away from the note.

"Not talking to her sooner. She's like my sister." She wrapped her arms around his waist. He loved the feeling of holding her.

"Then she understood why you held off on telling her until after she got back from her honeymoon?"

"Of course." She sighed against his chest. She was silent for a while. "We didn't use protection."

He stilled. "When?"

"Last night and this morning," she said.

He chuckled. "I can't speak for you, but I did. You must have been too far gone in lust to notice." He pulled back and smiled down at her. "I guess that's the ego boost I needed."

She frowned. "But… I… I didn't see you put…"

He smiled. "I never forget protection." He kissed her on her nose. "Trust me."

She nodded. "So, I don't need to stop off at the employee store and get any rubbers?"

He chuckled. "If it makes you feel better to have your own stash around."

"I had a few things I needed anyway." She sighed. "I'm sorry about not telling you that the Robinson group was staying on."

"I'll deal with it." He wrapped his arms around her again. "But I might be late tonight. I'll have to move some things around to accommodate all the supplies."

"That's okay, I have a few things to tie up here too."

"I'll swing by after…"

"No, I'll just meet you upstairs." She rubbed her hands up and down his back. He wanted to stretch into them like a cat, then spend the rest of the day snuggling with her, naked, locked together.

"Okay, I shouldn't be too long after dinner. Maybe we can take another walk?" he suggested.

"In the rain?"

He glanced out the window and frowned. "Sorry, forgot. There aren't any windows in the kitchen."

She smiled. "We can sit out on the porch and neck. You know, to further our cause." Her smile fell away when she remembered the new note.

He pulled her close. "Now that is a plan." He rubbed his lips across hers. "I'm looking forward to spending the night with you, in my bed."

She nodded her head slightly, then licked her lips, causing him to want to kiss them once more. Instead, he backed away, knowing he had to spend the next few hours trying to figure out menus and orders for the three days and fifty guests.

Then something else dawned on him as he walked towards the door. Turning back towards her, he asked. "Is that man staying on?" Her eyebrows shot up in question. "The one that was in here?"

"Tristen Robinson?" she supplied. He nodded quickly, his temper flaring. "Yes, but I told him I was seeing someone." Her face paled slightly. "There is no way he left the note." She crossed her arms over her chest.

"You've talked to him?" he asked, fisting his hands.

"He's a guest, and he apologized for yesterday." She sat down behind the desk. "He did not leave those notes," she said again.

"Even if he didn't, he didn't have the right to paw you—"

"Adam," she broke into his rant. "He was drunk, and he apologized. Besides, like I said, I told him we were involved."

That stopped his temper cold. "You did?"

She nodded and smiled. "I thought that was our plan."

He stormed over and leaned across her desk and planted another kiss on her lips. "Later." He wasn't sure if it was a promise or a threat. Without another word, he walked out of the office, his shoulders back, his head a little higher.

He was in love. There was no question about it. Not anymore. Now all he had to do was tell Lilly. Just that thought had his stomach rolling and his palms sweating.

CHAPTER 11

*L*ilith watched Adam leave the room and couldn't stop smiling for the next few hours while she made some calls and rearranged schedules. The note she'd discovered was all but forgotten.

She added three more people to the cleaning staff's schedule. She knew Adam would take care of the wait staff and kitchen personnel.

Rodney, the groundskeeper, informed her that there was still plenty to do during the rain and he would keep his staff busy enough. They had been in the process of cleaning all the gutters and power washing all the buildings before the rain started, but it would have to be put on hold until the rains stopped.

She had always loved the old gardener. He'd been working at East Haven since long before Sarah had even been born. Long before Sarah's father had even purchased the island resort. Rodney always joked that he was born to work there and would be there until the day he died.

Which, from the looks of him, should have been years

ago. But even though he looked frail and old, Lilith knew that wasn't the case. She'd had a hard time keeping up with the man when she'd worked under him. Even Rodney's grandson complained about how hard his grandfather worked him. The kid did like to complain. But so, did a lot of her staff.

She glanced down when her stomach growled. Picking up the phone, she decided to call down to the kitchen and order up an early dinner, but then hung up instead when she remembered that Adam was going to bring something up later.

She needed to get up and stretch her legs anyway. As she walked down the hallway, she thought of all the things that still had to be done that evening before she could spend time with Adam.

She was almost to the stairs when she noticed the door to the attic cracked open. The workers weren't supposed to be in there until the next morning. Stepping into the darkness, she called out.

"Hello?" Since the sky had turned dark already, there was no light shining through the window like it had at lunch. Searching for a light switch, she stubbed her toe on a box and cursed under her breath. "Is someone in here?" she called again after flipping on the dim light.

Nothing. Turning back to the door, she flipped the light off and shut the door behind her. Maybe a guest had wandered in by accident and had forgotten to shut the door all the way.

Her stomach growled again, causing her to rush down the stairs. She tripped at the bottom stair and would have landed face first if a strong hand hadn't caught her.

"Seems like I'm always catching you," Adam joked.

"Very funny." She stood up and straightened her dress. "Did we leave the attic door open?" she asked, glancing back up the stairs.

"No, I remember closing it behind you." He frowned down at her.

"Is that for me?" she asked, seeing the tray of food in his hands.

"For us." He smiled. "I pulled some strings to get a few minutes with you before the dinner rush." He glanced up the stairs. "Want to head back up?"

She sighed. "No, let's go out on the back porch and watch the rain." She followed him down the back hallway and held the door open for him.

Gone was the soft rain of earlier. Now it was falling in buckets. The lightning and wind kicked up too, causing them to have to sit near the back wall so they wouldn't get wet.

"I guess it's a good thing the Robinsons stuck around. Can you imagine being stuck out in a boat in this stuff?" she said, shoveling a piece of chicken and spicy noodles into her mouth.

"I've done that once in my life." He shivered. "No, thank you. I preferred to watch it from here."

"What happened?" She turned slightly towards him.

"I was taking my gran out on a sunny day and things took a quick turn. Let's just say we stick close to the shore-line now."

"Was she okay?"

Adam chuckled. "Actually, she enjoyed it. Laughed the entire time. I was sure she'd gone insane, but then she told me a story of when her father took her out in his fishing boat. They lived in Sète, a small fishing community off the southern coast of France, near the Mediterranean Sea. One day, she'd begged her father to take her along for the day. She was in her early teens and told her father she was old enough to learn the ropes. He took her and later that afternoon there was a big *orage*." He glanced at her. "Storm." He smiled.

"I would have remembered the word." She sighed and thought about brushing up on her French.

"Anyway, the fishing boat, *La Grande Dame*…" He glanced at her.

"The grand lady," she supplied, feeling accomplished.

"That was an easy one," he teased. "So, *La Grande Dame* was pulled out deep into the Balearic Sea, its dark waters taking them further and further away from home as the skies grew black."

She noticed that his accent grew thicker as he got more into the story. Even the sounds of the rain and thunder helped her picture how a young teenage girl would feel, lost, being tossed around in the dark waters.

"Soon, just when they were about to lose hope, the sky opened up and a bright light pointed to the most beautiful thing my mémère had ever seen."

"What?" She hadn't realized she was almost leaning over the table and straightened up. "What did they see?"

"Home." He leaned back. "Imagine seeing a hill, shown in light, covered with colorful buildings, surrounded by crystal teal waters, boats bobbing in the port. It must have looked like heaven." He sighed.

"You're a romantic." She chuckled. "I supposed I should have known that about you already, but…" She shook her head. "You put on this show, this façade. Angry Frenchman." He smiled.

"And? How is this harmful? My employees fear me enough to never question my judgment or slack off." His accent grew thicker. "Besides, life would be boring on the island if I didn't give them something to talk about behind closed doors."

"Is that why you angered me so much?" she asked.

"No." He glanced out at the rain. "I had other reasons."

"And?" She moved closer to him until her shoulder touched his. "What would those be?"

His hand reached under the table and took hers, then he lifted it until he brushed a kiss across her knuckles. "It is how we act."

"We?" she asked. "All French?"

"No." He frowned slightly. "I mean…" He took a deep breath. "Can we…"

She waited. She could tell he was flustered, but she needed to understand. "Did you like me? I mean, is that how you showed it?"

He shrugged. "I'd better…" He started to get up, but she held him in place.

"You don't have to irritate me so much to show me you like me." She took his face into her hands and leaned over to place a soft kiss on his lips. "Just tell me."

He dropped his forehead to hers and sighed. "Words are hard sometimes. Other times, they come out wrong."

She smiled. "Then show me." Her eyes met his. "But later. Right now, I have to go smooth over a few things."

He nodded, then pulled her in for a slow kiss. "Later." This time when he said it, she felt a shiver of excitement race through her.

He walked her back towards the stairs, then disappeared down the back way towards the kitchen. She took the next hour making sure everything was ready for the new guests. Instead of holding a birthday party outside by the pool house, the party would be moved into the dining room, which meant the Robinson family would have to eat lunch tomorrow somewhere else. Too bad the attic wasn't ready.

After clearing the morning room and having the staff move a few things around, they made enough room for a dozen people, which meant the Robinson clan would have to eat lunch in shifts. She doubted that was going to be acceptable since the group liked to socialize with one another.

She made her way up to the second floor and knocked on Tristen's door. His mother answered, dressed as if she was ready to visit the Queen herself.

Her long flowing evening dress made Lilith remember that she was still in her simple sundress.

"Evening. I understand you're getting ready for dinner but wondered if you had a moment to talk?" she asked.

"Sure, come in." The woman moved aside. "You're the manager, correct?"

"Yes, ma'am. I'm Lilith Brown."

"What can I do for you?" She motioned for her to take a seat. Lilith moved over and sat on the settee.

"Well, it's about lunch tomorrow. Our new guests will be occupying the dining room for their party, which had to be moved from the pool area to indoors due to the weather," she started.

"And where do you expect our group will dine?" Mrs. Robinson broke in.

"We've arranged enough room in the morning room

for a dozen to eat comfortably. We would have to take you in shifts, though."

"Well, I suppose if it's just for one day. I'll speak to everyone." The woman looked irritated, then stood up. "If that's all…"

"Yes." She stood to go.

"You know; I appreciate the way you handled my son the other day." Her eyes bore into hers.

"Oh?" She stopped, her hand on the door handle.

"Tristen can be… a little wild. It's one of the reasons we're set on marrying him to Kaleen. Her family is well established." The woman's eyes roamed over her simple cotton dress. "They would make a good match."

Lilith's shoulders straightened. "I'm sure they would. Good evening." She nodded, then stepped out into the hallway.

Once outside, she took a deep breath. Why would anyone want to be wound up so tight? She headed down to the main dining room to make sure everything was perfect for an oversized dinner group.

She stuck around until guests started arriving, then stepped into the hallway towards the back staircase, only to be stopped by the pretty brunette.

"I understand you've been talking to Tristen," Kaleen said. The woman's evening gown was even more exquisite than Tristen's mothers had been. Its emerald green material shined in the dim light of the hallway.

"I speak to all of my guests, it's my job." She waited patiently as the woman's face went from kind to twisted.

"I don't appreciate women trying to throw themselves on him. I understand a lot of…"—her eyes moved up and down her sundress— "women think that simply because he's famous and a member of one of the richest families in the States, that they can throw themselves at him. I'm a very jealous woman. I won't stand for it, nor will his family. I've already had a talk with his parents and they are quite aware of your… behavior."

Lilith held in a smile. "I assure you, it won't happen again." She tried to step around the woman, only to have her arm grabbed in a surprisingly strong grip.

"See that it doesn't, or I will have you fired." She waited until Lilith nodded slightly, then dropped her arm and walked away.

Oh, there were times in her life where she desperately wished she could speak her mind. Either that or punch someone square in the nose. Taking several cleansing breaths, she moved on to complete her normal evening rounds before heading back upstairs to check on the rest of the staff. Then she swung back by the office and was relieved to see that the attic door was shut tight.

She spent the next hour pouring over new orders for the laundry service, setting schedules for staff members, and trying to create a plan for the new attic ballroom. She knew that, on occasions such as tomorrow's lunch, the large room upstairs could double as a dining room. Then her mind turned to the practical side of having wait staff climb three flights of stairs with trays of food and drinks. She wanted to have a full bar built along one wall but wondered how practical the rest would be.

Then she remembered the old dumbwaiter in the current dining room, the one that Tom Elliott, the last general manager of the resort, had updated.

She was so curious whether there was a dumbwaiter in

the attic room that she logged out of the computer and headed into the ballroom to check.

She wished instantly that she had changed out of her cream dress since she figured she'd have to move several piles of boxes just to check each wall.

First, she looked against the wall with the window. Doubting it would be there, she made a quick sweep. Then she moved to the wall on the left, the most likely location. If it wasn't there, she wondered if Sarah had plans to the place somewhere, so she could see about having one installed. Of course, that would cut heavily into the budget she'd already worked out.

She had talked to Sarah a few weeks back about the budget of the resort and knew there was an extra ten thousand dollars left over. She planned on using only a portion of it for the cleanup.

She had pushed most of the boxes away from the walls and was excited to see one wall completely covered with intricate wood paneling. She could just imagine a massive wood bar along the wall. It was a little too dark to see if there were any major repairs needed or if the paneling just needed a fresh coat of stain.

Moving on, she walked across the floor to the other wall and started pulling the heavy furniture aside. Glancing down at her watch, she figured she had about an hour before Adam would get off his shift. Just enough time to tackle clearing this wall.

She moved a large table that had been stacked high with boxes away from the back wall. When she moved aside a large wardrobe, she smiled. There was a door. Dusting off her hands, she opened it and reached inside for a switch.

She walked into a small room, and there in the back was the dumbwaiter she'd been searching for. It didn't look like it was in working order, but at least it was here. Glancing around, she realized the room had once been used for food staging. At one point, the attic had served as a ballroom.

Her excitement level spiked. Then she heard a light creaking sound and her heart stilled. Her head spun around to the doorway and she watched it slowly swing closed by itself.

She laughed at herself for jumping at shadows. The door was clearly in need of oil and had just shut by itself.

Walking over, she reached for the handle and frowned when it didn't budge. Then true panic set in and everything in the logical side of her brain shut down.

Adam climbed the three flights of stairs and felt every sore muscle in his body. Most people thought that being a chef was an easy job, but he was on his feet all day, usually standing over a hot stove, unloading and loading heavy crates of food. And that didn't include the cleanup detail.

But with every sore muscle came the reminder that he was doing what he loved. In a place that he loved.

He'd done some digging into the new note. It appeared that the green notepaper was not stocked in the employees' store. Which could just mean that someone had bought it from the mainland. The writing was blocked and in Sharpie. Nothing really stood out other than it pissed him off.

He knew from experience that Sarah's office door was

always locked. He had a key, so he could deliver invoices once a day, and if Sarah wasn't there, he could leave them in her inbox. There were three others besides him on the island that had a key: Lilly, Rodney, and Heather. He couldn't see Rodney or Heather as being the person who'd written the notes or trashed her room.

As he reached the top of the stairs, his phone rang. Seeing his father's number on the screen, he groaned. Just one more thing he had to deal with today.

"Bonjour, Papa." He held in a sigh when his father started in on him immediately. Why didn't he move to Bordeaux, closer to them? His father could pull some strings and get him a job in financing with a local winery.

His family may be old and high in politics, but there was no way he wanted to get pushed into a career just because he was his father's son. He spent the next few minutes politely declining and explaining himself while his father's voice grew angrier.

His father's calls had become more frequent. His mother still called once a month and sounded more and more unhappy with each conversation. He'd visited them last Christmas, before taking the job at East Haven. But, still, he wondered if another trip was in order.

Maybe his mother was having health issues? His father had hinted at visits to the doctor, but he'd assumed instantly that it had been his father. Maybe his Nana knew more?

Deciding to swing by and talk to her before heading back to the island tomorrow evening to set their trap, he pushed his family to the back of his mind and walked into his room, only to find it empty.

He turned back to the hallway and stormed down to her

door. When there was no answer, he headed back out into the rain to the main building to see if she was still up in the office.

When he found that room empty as well, he walked through the dining room, asking every employee if they had seen her.

Some had seen her a few hours ago, making her normal evening rounds. After that, everyone thought she had disappeared upstairs into Sarah's office.

Pulling out his cell phone, he tried her number for the hundredth time as he made his way up the stairs. When he reached the top, he heard her ringtone and rushed to the office, only to find it empty and her phone sitting under some papers on the desk.

He sat down as sheer panic washed over him. For as long as he'd known Lilly, he'd never been seen her without the phone in her hand or a pocket.

Where would she have gone? What was she working on? Did the person responsible for the break-in and for leaving the note have something to do with this? Fear caused his hands to shake as he reached for the house phone and dialed the main desk.

"Stacey, Lilly is missing, have you seen her?"

"Lilly? You mean Lilith?"

"Yes," he growled, feeling the worry grow. "Her phone is in the office, but she's not here or in the employees' building.

"She talked about stopping off at the store."

"The employees'?"

"Yes, she needed a few things."

He remembered their conversation about the rubbers and felt relief wash over him. "I'll check down there."

"Okay, I'll keep my eye out for her."

"Thanks." He hung up and rushed from the room, taking her phone with him.

He rushed through the rain, getting soaked this time and not caring. He pulled open the large shed door, and Nate, Rodney's grandson was in there, a cigarette hanging from his mouth and several candy bars in his hands.

"Hey." He looked around as if guilty.

"Have you seen Lilith?" He took a step closer.

Nate dropped the candy bars down on the shelf and shrugged. "I was going to pay for 'em, I swear."

"I don't give a damn about the candy bars," he growled. "Have you seen Lilith?"

"No man. I've been busy today." He puffed out smoke towards him. "Besides, I think the lady can…"

Adam ignored the kid and walked over to find the clipboard that held the honor system's docket. Basic grocery items lined the shelves on either wall. The cost of each item taken would later be deducted from each person's paycheck.

Adam scanned the names and items as he heard Nate leave. He noted the last time Lilly took anything from the store was three days ago.

Slamming the clipboard down, he ran back to the main building and started once more rushing around to each employee. This time he enlisted a few of his staff who had finished up their night shift to help him look for her, but none of them found a trace of her.

An hour later, he called the police as he sat in the office.

"What do you mean you can't help us?" He almost screamed it into the phone. "She's missing!"

"We can't file a report until…"

"You said that already. What about sending someone out here to help look for her?" He thought about boats, helicopters, search dogs.

"I'm sorry, sir. Have you tried to look for her yourself?"

"Of course, we have." He looked around the room at the other concerned faces.

After another moment of listening to the woman's explanation that they had to wait to file a report, he hung up the phone.

Standing up quickly, he walked over to the window and stared out into the darkness. Then for some reason, he remembered the note in his back pocket. He'd been so concerned with finding Lilly, he hadn't thought about it

"What about Tristen Robinson?" someone said, breaking into his thoughts and causing him to turn around and frown at the group.

"What about him?" he asked, feeling his heart skip.

"Well, it's just…" Carmen, the head housekeeper, glanced down at her hands. "I saw them talking today, in the dining room."

"And?" It came out as a growl.

"Well, I overheard him the other day talking to his friends. He seemed very interested in Lilith," she said, glancing towards the door. "He's in room Two-oh-eight. It wouldn't hurt to check."

He stood up. "Keep looking. Check every room again," he said and then left the room without another word. When he knocked on the door, he was even more determined than before.

A man in his early fifties answered, dressed in silk pajamas and looking very annoyed at the interruption.

"I'm sorry to bother you, but one of our staff members has gone missing and…" He glanced over the man's shoulder and saw the younger man standing behind his father. "When was the last time you saw Lilith?" he demanded, ignoring the other man.

"I haven't seen her since earlier today."

"I talked with the young woman just before dinner." A woman stepped into view. Her long white nightgown flowed around her as she tied a robe around her waist. "Has something happened to her?"

"We aren't sure. We're trying to figure it out. Do you have any ideas where she headed after you talked to her?"

"I saw her in the dining room as we arrived for dinner. After that, I'm afraid I don't know," the woman said, walking over and laying a hand on her husband.

"Kaleen said she had a word with her," Tristen added. "Maybe she told her her plans?"

"Which room?"

"Her family is next door," the woman supplied. "Why don't I go with you. It might smooth things over a little."

This time, when he knocked, he kept it gentle. Lilith would want him to remember these were paying guests.

When the door opened, he allowed Tristen's mother to speak, then waited in the hallway as Kaleen was woken. They waited almost ten minutes. Finally, a short brunette opened the door, a crimson robe wrapped loosely around her waist.

The woman looked like she had taken the time to comb her hair and apply makeup before coming to the door.

"Kaleen, dear. I know it's late, but we were wondering if you spoke with…" Tristen's mother turned to him.

"Lilith Brown. She's the general manager."

"Yes, I know who she is." The woman crossed her arms over her ample chest. "I spoke with her about her appalling behavior towards my Tristen. I mean, the woman practically threw herself at him."

Adam held in a growl. "When I walked in on them the other day, the only one throwing themselves at the other was your Tristen. So much so that I had to restrain him," he added.

He heard the women gasp, which shook his mind clear. He had to focus. "When and where did you have this talk with her?"

Kaleen glared at him. "The hallway outside the dining room. Just before dinner." She lifted her chin. "If you're done, I'd like to get my beauty rest." She started to shut the door, but he put a hand up, holding it open.

"You didn't speak with her after that?"

"No, as I've said… that was the only time I've seen her today." She glared down at his hand until he removed it.

"Thank you," he said to Tristen's mother.

"I'm sorry about my son. I apologized to Miss Brown earlier about his behavior."

He nodded quickly, then started walking back down the long hallway. His head was aching as he climbed the stairs once more, unsure of his next move. As he passed the attic, he remembered her plans to have the place fixed up before Sarah's return.

Opening the heavy door, he walked in and noticed the lights were all on. Calling out, he waited and listened. Nothing. He called again; the room was massive.

He noticed several things had been moved. Large boxes, furniture, and even the table he had set up for lunch had been pulled aside. He rushed around the room, searching for… something. He didn't know what.

Then he heard a muffled cry and froze. He waited until the sound came again. Then he raced towards the back wall. He had to push aside a heavy wardrobe, but he found a door. Pushing it open, he looked into the room and saw a small white bundle huddled in the corner.

CHAPTER 12

*H*er mind had traveled through time and space, back to the time when she was young and didn't believe that she would ever survive each night.

Back when she was afraid of the dark, of every unexplained noise in the night. Scared of things she couldn't control, things she didn't fully understand, but knew were wrong.

The air in the small room she'd been locked in until her mother's return had grown stale and smelled of mold, sweat, and something else she didn't dare think of.

Each time she'd been locked away, she'd wondered if maybe this time they would forget about her and she would die down in the darkness. Her mind screamed that she should fight each time the door opened, but she knew better. The marks and bruises she'd gained from fighting had never stopped anything. Instead, she allowed her mind to slip into another world. One where she did what she wanted, grew tall and strong and learned how to protect herself. And no one ever touched her, unless she wanted them to.

Her body shook with the tears that slipped down her face, soaking her nightgown. Still, tears were better than the blood that sometimes covered her tiny body.

She tucked her body tight when she heard the door open, saw the light from the hallway. Her mind started to retreat into its safe place when she heard the softest words calling out her name. But this time, it wasn't Cara they were calling for, this time it was Lilly. The sweetest name she'd ever been called.

Her eyes slid open as warm, soft hands wrapped around her, holding her tight. More tears slid down her face as Adam's soft words comforted her.

"Lilly, my Lilly," he said over and over again as he held her tight.

"Adam?" Her mind snapped back to the present, her past leaving its bitter sting in the back of her mind. Her arms wrapped around him, holding him tighter than she'd ever held anything or anyone in her life.

She felt herself being lifted, carried out of the attic, down the bright hallway. She shut her eyes to the lights and enjoyed the feeling of being safe, far away from her past.

When he laid her down on a soft bed, she sighed and reached for him, but instead, she found empty air.

"Shh, I have to make a few calls. Then I'll take you to my room."

Her eyes flew open and she realized she was laying on the sofa in Sarah's office. She shivered again and watched Adam pull out his cell phone.

"I've found her." His eyes met hers. "The attic. I'll talk

to you later. I'm going to get her back to my room and take care of her." He paused. "Yes, okay. Thanks. Tell everyone else…" He smiled slightly. "Yes, thanks," he said again before hanging up.

"I'm sorry if I made you worry." Her eyes burned again. "The door must have shut behind me." She tried to remember what had actually happened, but all she could remember was the sheer panic of meeting a locked door and looking around to realize how small the room was. After that, everything else was a blur.

"It's okay." He moved back to her, then ran his hand down her face. "Why don't I take you back to my room. You can take a hot bath and tell me what happened."

It sounded so wonderful, she started to get up, but her legs were still shaking. He must have noticed because he reached down and picked her back up.

"I like this." She wrapped her arms around his neck.

"What?" he asked, smiling down at her. "Me carrying you? Or the attention?"

She frowned slightly. "You are carrying me."

He nodded. "Then I'll make a point to do it often." He pulled the office door shut behind him, then shifted her weight and headed towards the back staircase.

"You can hold the umbrella," he said, standing just inside the back door. When he leaned down, she reached out and took the umbrella and opened it.

The rain and wind were stronger now than before. "When is this supposed to end?" he asked, avoiding a large puddle of water.

"Wednesday. Then we can get back to our summer."

He smiled down at her. "I'll take you out on my boat."

"Really?" She already felt herself settling.

"Maybe Nana will come along. I know she's going to love you." He shifted and opened the door to the employees' building.

As he walked them up the stairs and down their hall, several people greeted them.

"You okay?" Heather brushed a strand of her hair aside.

"I'm fine, really." She felt foolish and suddenly wished she was walking instead of being carried by Adam.

"You're covered in dust and cobwebs." Heather brushed at her hair again.

"She's going to clean up in my room," Adam said loudly. A little too loud for her liking, but then she remembered their plan to catch whoever had broken into her room. Her skin chilled as she remembered the creak of a floorboard before the door shut behind her.

"Adam." Her voice sounded far away. "I'd like…"

He looked down at her and moved quickly into his room. He laid her down gently on the bed, then covered her with a blanket. "I'll start a bath."

"Hot," she whispered. "Boiling." She shivered and hugged the blanket tighter.

Adam nodded, then disappeared into his bathroom. She stared up at the ceiling and ran over everything from dinner on. What she'd done up in the attic to just before moving the wardrobe aside.

Then Adam walked back into the room. "Would you like some help?" He glanced down at her.

"No, I think I can manage." She took the blanket with her, shutting the bathroom door behind her. She quickly stripped off her dirty sundress and thought about throwing it in the waste bin. Instead, she folded it and hung it over his towel rack.

His bathroom was almost identical to hers but slightly smaller. She was happily surprised when she found a towel, exactly where she had hers. She even found some bubbles and poured them into the water, then slowly climbed in. The heat seeped through her cold skin, deeper into her bones. She had just relaxed into the water when she heard her cell phone ring.

She moved to get out, but Adam called into her.

"I'll get it. It's Sarah," he said, and she could hear him talking to her friend. "Yes, the attic. No, she's okay, just shaken." There was a pause. "In the closet up there." He chuckled. "Yes, there's a closet. Behind a wardrobe." Another pause. "I don't know. I'll keep you posted." A longer pause. "I'll have her call you in the morning." She heard him hang up and walk towards the door.

"Mind if I come in?" he called out.

Instantly, she felt shy, but then remembered what he had done to her last night. "Sure," she said weakly.

"Sure, you mind?" He smiled as he opened the door, his eyes instantly finding any exposed skin that wasn't covered by bubbles. She felt her face heat and desire shoot instantly through her.

All of Adam's anger, fear, and worry for Lilly disappeared the second he stepped into the bathroom and saw her relaxing in his bathtub. Her long hair was soaked, flowing over her shoulders, and her face was cleared of the dust and makeup that had run down her face before.

Her eyes looked heavy and when his eyes roamed lower, his body reacted to the sight of her soft skin hiding under the white bubbles and water.

"Are you alright?" he asked, afraid to move closer to her. She'd just been locked in the attic for several hours. He knew she needed some time to recover.

She nodded, then held out a hand. "There's enough room in here for two." She waved him towards her.

Instead, he walked over and sat on the edge. "How about I wash your back?" He smiled, believing that he would be able to keep himself in check if he kept his clothes on.

"I'd prefer you in here." She sat up and his eyes couldn't move away from the sight of the water and bubbles sliding down her perfect breasts.

"Lilly." His voice sounded odd, so he cleared his throat. "I… you need to…"

"Take your clothes off and get you in here with me," she finished, tugging on his shirt until he helped her pull it over his head. Then she threw it into the corner of the bathroom and started to tug on his pants.

His eyes were glued to her skin and he was sure he wasn't going to make it much longer without feeling her skin next to his. Standing up, he toed off his shoes, then yanked down his pants and pulled off his socks.

"Impressive." She smiled up at him. "I didn't really get a good look at you before." Her eyes moved up and down his body, causing him to grow even harder.

"Look all you want." His eyes moved slowly over her, then she leaned back and wiggled her finger towards him.

"Come, wash my back." She smiled.

He took a step towards her, then cursed under his

breath. Quickly moving over, he pulled a condom from his pocket and set it on the edge of the tub. "See," he smiled. "I come prepared."

"So, you do." Her eyes were glued on his hardness and he watched as her tongue darted out and licked her lips.

He moved quickly, tucking his hands under her arms and pulling her up until he could slide into the water behind her. She rested back against his chest, his hardness pressed against her softness as his hands roamed over every inch of her. His mouth trailed down her neck until he felt her shiver.

Slowly his fingers traveled over her soft skin, below the warm water, and disappeared into her silky folds, causing her hips to move with his rhythm.

"You're so soft," he said between kisses. "So perfect, here." He touched his fingertips to the spot he wanted. "And here." He moved his fingers to a new spot and heard her moan. "There?" he asked, watching her eyes flutter closed as she nodded. "How about here?" He moved again and heard her gasp and jerk under the water.

"Yes," she groaned. "More," she begged.

He dipped his finger deeper and this time it was his turn to close his eyes and moan. "You're so tight, so ready for me." He knew he wanted to show her slowness, like before, but the thought of losing her was still so fresh on his mind.

Reaching back, he slid on the condom and lifted her hips until she fit him like a glove. "Move with me," he said against her shoulder.

Then she did. Her hips rotated, jerked with desire, and he wrapped his arms around her, his hands cupping her softness as she enjoyed herself.

Water splashed over the edge of the tub, and the rhythm and sound of it was exciting in itself. Her nails dug into his thighs as she held herself over him, moving slowly to her own internal beat.

"Adam?" She rolled her head back. He pushed her wet hair aside, then laid his lips softly underneath her ear and nibbled lightly.

Then she was pulling away, turning until her legs went around his hips and she was once more wrapped around him. Her soft breasts pushed tight against his chest, her mouth fused with his as her hips continued to move.

She was driving him mad. He was under her complete control, pinned to the bottom of the tub, held still by the soft curves of her body.

There was no other place he'd rather be than right there, with her. He felt his body tense as he felt hers soften around him. Moments before she cried out his name, he felt himself lose his heart. He lost the battle of trying to hide his feelings for her and whispered next to her ear the three words he'd never said before in his life.

CHAPTER 13

*L*illy relaxed against Adam's chest and couldn't stop smiling. Even though her heartbeat had returned to normal, her mind was still whirling.

"You know; I think I needed that." She giggled.

"Hmm?" He groaned, his hands still rubbing her back in slow circles.

"Hearing you say that." She leaned up and looked down at him. When her hair fell forward, she pushed it aside. His hand came up and helped her, holding the long tresses back.

"I wouldn't mind hearing them back." His eyes held hers.

"When I was locked in"—she took a breath— "I sort of lost my mind." He waited, his hand gently rubbing her hair and back. "I flashed back to all the times Dave would lock me in the laundry room until he came for me again." She shivered, causing him to lean forward and wrap his arms around her. "Then, I heard you calling me Lilly." She closed her eyes and smiled. "I love you, Adam. You gave me something no one else ever has."

"What's that?" he said after placing a soft kiss on her shoulder.

"Something more beautiful than I've ever seen. A name that matches my heart." She felt a tear slide down her face, then leaned back and took his face into her hands. "I love you, Adam." She repeated. "I love who I am to you. Your Lilly."

He smiled and leaned up to place a kiss on her lips. Then in one swift move, he pulled her up and carried her from the bath, almost slipping along the way.

She laughed and held onto him. "That's how I imagine most bathroom accidents happen," she said once he'd laid her on the bed.

"I suppose I need a few more rugs on the tile floor." He grinned down at her and then wrapped a hand around her thigh and slid slowly into her again. "Later," he said, coming down to cover her lips with his once more.

She allowed her mind and body to completely lose track once more, only this time, he was her anchor to the present.

She woke with a jolt to the clash of thunder, her entire body tense from the nightmare she'd been having. Strong arms wrapped around her gently and she instantly relaxed back against Adam's chest.

"Qu'est-ce qui ne va pas, mon amour?" Adam's voice was slurred, and she noticed his accent had grown thicker.

"Hmm?" She turned slightly towards him, enjoying the feel of his warm chest against hers. Somehow, she was once more freezing.

"What's wrong?" he asked in English.

"Nightmare," she said against his chest. "It's over now."

His hand brushed down her hair and tilted her head back, so he could look into her eyes even in the darkness.

"Is it because you're claustrophobic?"

"No, I don't really mind small spaces, as long as there's a way out." She sighed, then could feel her entire body tense. "My stepdad would lock me in the laundry room until…"

He touched his lips with hers. "Don't. I understand." He brushed his lips against hers. "Let's leave it for the daylight. Now, this is our time." His lips warmed her body slowly as his hands found every spot that sent shivers of excitement rushing through her.

"Let go," he said next to her skin. "I want to feel you take what you want." He settled between her legs. She wrapped them around his hips, holding him closer to her. Her back arched off of the mattress as he slid into her.

They made love slowly as the lightning lit up the room around them and the sound of the thunder went unnoticed.

The next time she woke up, it was to the sound of soft rain outside. Adam's arms were wrapped around her and his alarm was going off.

"Just ignore it," he said into her hair.

"What kind of boss would I be if I let you show up to work late?" she joked as she started to get up.

His arms held her into place and she felt her stomach growl. "Besides, I'm starving." His arms dropped, and she rolled out of the bed. She grabbed up the loose sheet and wrapped it around her as she made her way to the restroom.

She took her time in the shower, then tried to clean off

her dress enough that she could head back to her room to change for the day. It was pretty much a lost cause, but still, she tried.

When there was a knock on the door, she opened it up and smiled when Adam was there, holding a new outfit for her.

"I figured you could use a few things from your room." He handed her a pair of black slacks, a teal blouse, and a matching pair of shoes. "I… uh"—he handed her the overnight bag she had— "grabbed a few other things." He nodded. "I'm not really good…" He actually blushed.

She leaned against the door, her eyebrows rose. "What is it about packing my…"—she glanced in the bag and saw her makeup bag, some bras and panties, and a brush— "makeup that makes you blush?"

He eyes darkened. "I never blush." His accent was thicker, causing her to laugh.

Then she remembered what was hiding in her underwear drawer and it was her turn to blush. Shutting the door in his face as he laughed at her realization, she leaned her forehead against the door.

"I won it at Sarah's bachelorette party."

"Sure, you did," he joked behind the door.

"Really." She closed her eyes and took several deep breaths.

She heard him chuckle as he walked away.

When she walked out, he was sitting at his computer. He turned to her and smiled. "You look fresher today."

"I feel much better." She walked over and kissed him squarely on his lips just as her phone rang. "Ugh, it starts," she said, seeing Sarah's face on her screen.

"She was worried sick about you." He shut down his

computer and opened his door. "I'll give you some privacy."

She waved him away as she answered the phone.

"Talk," Sarah said.

"Good morning," she said cheerfully.

"Well, someone got some last night, but that's not why I called. I want to hear what happened to you."

"I got locked in a closet in the attic. No big deal."

"Why were you in the attic?"

Lilith paused. "We've had to extend the Robinson's stay, due to weather, and I needed a few extra chairs." She hated lying to her friend. "Anyway, I walked into the closet up there. I guess the door needs some work because it shut behind me."

"Why was it locked?"

"I don't know, but I'm planning to have someone take a look at it today." That much was true. Glancing down at her watch, she realized she had less than an hour before the crew was supposed to arrive to start working up there. Heading out Adam's door, she flipped the lock and made sure to shut the door firmly behind her, tugging on it to make sure it was secure.

Then she headed down the hall as she listened to Sarah.

"Sounds good. Whatever they need to do. Are you okay?" She heard the worry in her friend's voice.

"I am now." She sighed as she reached the bottom of the stairs and opened the umbrella. "It's still raining here. What about there?" She knew she was changing the subject but didn't feel like going too deep into how freaked out she'd been.

"It's beautiful here. We're went paragliding yesterday.

It was amazing. I thought we'd be jumping off a cliff, but really, we just walked off the side of a mountain and the paraglider just lifted us up gently. It was like we were floating on a cloud. There was a rainbow and we actually went right through it!" Sarah's voice turned excited, then dreamy. "Ben's a little afraid of heights, but he absolutely loved going. We're going to try to schedule another trip before we leave. Today, we're going snorkeling at Black Rock Beach. I've never been snorkeling before. Ben says I'll love it. He's going to try to convince me to jump off the cliff's there, into the water. It's a fifteen-foot drop. I'm not sure if I will."

Lilith giggled as she stepped onto the back porch of the main house and shook her umbrella clear of water. "Do it. If you can walk off of the side of a mountain and paraglide, then you should be able to jump off a rock into the water."

"Cliff. It's a cliff."

She giggled. "I'm sure you'll love it. It sounds more like an adventure than a honeymoon."

"Both." Sarah's voice turned dreamy. "Sounds like you and Adam are getting chummy."

"Later," she warned. "Right now, I have to go be a boss."

"Are you enjoying it? Or are you hating me for leaving you in charge."

She thought about it for a moment. "Both."

Sarah laughed. "Fair enough. If you need—"

"Nope," she broke in. "You go swim with the fishes. Send me some pictures. I've never been snorkeling in Hawaii."

"I'll send you some today. Thanks, Lil."

"Anytime." She felt her eyes water. "Thank you."

"For?"

"Being my sister," she choked out.

There was silence on the line. "Now you've gone and done it. You've made me cry on my honeymoon."

"Then hang up and go have fun with your husband."

"That I can do." She heard Sarah blow a kiss and then hang up.

After a quick fruit bowl for breakfast, Lilith made her way up the stairs and waited for the workers to arrive. The rain continued to drizzle outside, causing most of the guests to remain indoors. Which, she quickly found out, was driving her employees nuts.

She'd never met a more demanding group of people. In the last two days' she'd heard a complaint from every single employee about the group. The new guests were quiet and reserved where the Robinson clan was quickly becoming louder and more boisterous. She'd even broken in on a few arguments in the dining hall before she'd headed upstairs.

When the workers finally arrived, she quickly laid out her plans and showed them the storage room where she wanted everything moved to. She had planned on going through the boxes herself to see if there was anything useful, so as the men hauled them into the storage room, she spent her time looking in them and separating what could be useful.

By lunchtime, she was thankful Adam had picked the darker slacks for her to wear. She dusted her hands and decided to eat lunch down in the kitchen instead of the office.

The workers had cleared the entire attic and she swung

by there to check it out as they started sanding and worked on retaining some of the wood.

The crew sat in the corner, eating the sack lunches she had brought up from the kitchen.

"It's coming along," she said, nodding to them.

The room was easily double the size of the main dining room. She thought about purchasing some folding round tables and thought they could easily be stored in the closet she'd been locked in yesterday. She avoided glancing towards the door and avoided that corner of the room altogether.

The window was one of the nicest features of the room. There was a small fireplace along one wall that she had seen the day before. It would need some work.

When her stomach growled again, she headed downstairs to the kitchen and found Adam holding an employee against the wall in a death grip. His face was red and she'd never seen him so angry before. Several other employees stood back, watching in horror.

Adam's morning had gone from wonderful to terrible quickly. It had started when he'd journeyed into Lilly's room to gather some items for her to dress in.

He'd found the green piece of paper sitting directly inside her door like it had been pushed under.

His fingers had fisted, and he'd felt like throwing it, but held off and turned it over slowly instead.

"Stop it! Last warning."

He thought about showing Lilly but then remembered

how she'd looked last night and decided to keep it to himself. He would call the police back and talk to them.

He was due to leave the island around noon and planned to swing by the police station himself and show them the notes.

When he'd walked out of his room, leaving Lilly alone to talk with Sarah, he had bumped solidly into one of the men who had been top on the list of suspects.

Rob was one of his best sous chefs, however, the man was single and a little creepy when it came to talk about his personal life. No one knew if he was seeing someone or just lying about all the women he did see. Every time he came back from his time off, he would brag about all the hookups he'd had.

Adam knew for a fact that the man's room was on the next floor down. He reached out and took the man's arm.

"Is there something you want?"

"Hey, man," Rob said, stopping. "Sorry for bumping into you."

"What are you doing on this floor?" Adam demanded.

Rob's eyes searched around, then he smiled. "Guess I just got lost."

Adam moved towards him, but then the door next to them opened and Heather stepped out, a towel wrapped around her and her hair wet.

"Were you going to leave without saying goodbye?" She glared at Rob, who looked guilty.

Then Adam realized that the man's shirt was on inside out and that he was obviously unshaven for the morning. Adam dropped his arm and stepped away as Rob moved towards Heather.

"Oh, come on baby. I never say goodbye." He leaned

in and placed a soft kiss on Heather's waiting lips. Then she pulled Rob back into her doorway and winked at Adam. "I'll make sure he's on time, boss man."

Adam tried to hold in a chuckle, but the worry had built up about trying to find whoever had locked Lilly in the closet yesterday. He hadn't even mentioned the fact that there was no way that the door had just closed by itself and the wardrobe had magically moved back in front of the doorway.

As the morning shift started, his eyes and ears were open to everything. He could only watch his staff in the kitchen, but that didn't mean he wouldn't make sure it wasn't one of his crew.

His mind played over and over the list in his mind. Who had been around yesterday? Who hadn't?

He only had until noon before he had to pretend to leave the island. The weather had yet to let up and he knew that sneaking back onto the island would prove a little more challenging than he'd first expected.

He even thought about canceling his time off but knew that it would only postpone finding out who was doing this to Lilly.

It was just before lunch that he overheard several of his wait staff talking about how Lilly had been locked in the attic.

He stood around the corner from the two men and overheard them talking.

"If you ask me, she did it for attention. I mean, women are always doing crazy stuff like that to get attention. The last girlfriend I had tried to convince me she was pregnant just to get me to marry her."

"What happened?" the other man asked.

"I ditched the bitch when she started bleeding again."
He chuckled. "It wouldn't surprise me if Lilith locked
herself away just to get Adam to sleep with her. God
knows she'd need to do something drastic to get my
attention."

"She's not your type?" the other one asked.

"Are you kidding me? I like my women with less meat
on them. If they can't be on the cover of Playboy, I don't
even bother."

Adam felt his temper spike. Lilly was perfect. More
beautiful than any woman he'd ever seen. He could
remember the first time he'd seen her. He'd actually felt
his heart skip when the sun had settled on her hair.

"Besides, I've been here for almost five years. If you
ask me, I think she's a dyke waiting to happen. She's just
stringing Adam along because he's the boss."

Adam's temper hit an all-time high. Before he knew
what, he was doing, he rushed around the corner and had
the man in a headlock.

"Adam!" Lilly's voice sounded somewhere in the back
of his mind.

"If you ever talk about Lilly like that again," he
growled out lowly.

"Sorry, man," the guy said as he let him go.

"You're fired," he barked out, only to have Lilly step
between them.

"No, he's not. Shane, why don't you take a break."

"Yes, he is," Adam scolded, turning to her.

"No." Lilly turned to him. "Hiring and firing falls
under my title. I'd be happy to discuss this further with
you in my office." She turned to the man. Adam squinted
his eyes at him, causing the guy to take a step back.

"Shane, go, take your break."

"I didn't mean anything." He shrugged. "You know me; I like to talk."

"I understand. Go. I'll talk with you later." She turned to him. "Upstairs. Now," she said under her breath.

"I have lunch…" He turned away, the anger still vibrating through him.

"Then after." She walked out of the room without another word.

He turned back to all his employees. "Back to work," he growled, then stormed to his office and slammed the door.

Damn it, he was just trying to protect her. If that ass, Shane, talked behind her back, what was to stop him from… He closed his eyes and took several deep breaths.

Really, the kid hadn't done anything that Adam hadn't done himself at one point. Gossip. Especially about women. Actually, before he'd started seeing Lilly, he'd said and done a few things in front of her himself that he was ashamed of.

"Damn," he said to the empty room. He realized he was going to have to apologize.

CHAPTER 14

It took several minutes for Lilly to calm down. She leaned against the office door and took several deep breaths. She played out exactly what she was going to say to Adam once he came upstairs.

She ignored her growling stomach and sat behind the desk finishing some work until she heard the knock on the door.

"Come in," she called out. She was surprised that it was Carl, the officer from the mainland, who stood outside her door.

"Hi, Lilith. I hate to bug you at work," he said.

"It's not a bother." She stood up. "Please, come in."

Carl walked in and shut the door behind him.

"Please." She motioned for him to sit down.

He walked over and sat down. "I'm here about your case."

Her eyebrows shot up. "My…"

"The break-in."

"Yes." With everything else that had gone on in the last

few days, she'd completely forgotten about her room being destroyed. "Have you found anything?"

"I'm afraid not," he said, leaning forward. "I'm here to ask you a few more questions."

"Okay." She leaned forward, her elbows on the desk, while Carl pulled out a pad and pen. She thought about how a few months ago she would have considered going out with the man sitting across from her. He was good-looking enough, around her age and, to her knowledge, single. He'd even asked her out a few times, but she'd never really thought about dating, that was until Adam had come into town.

"There's a rumor going around that you and the chef…"—he glanced down at his notes— "Carriveau, have recently started seeing one another."

She felt her head start to ache. "Yes. How is this pertinent to the break-in?"

He glanced up at her. "We're just checking on every lead."

"I was with Adam the night someone broke in," she supplied.

Carl's dark eyebrows rose. "The entire night?"

She blinked. "No, but all before then. Before the break-in, I mean. He couldn't have snuck into my room and messed it up since I was with him."

He leaned back, crossing his leg over the other. "I remember when you moved into town." He smiled slightly.

She was thrown off for just a moment, then sighed. "I came in with a bus full of people."

"You'd been evacuated from the south." She nodded. "Katrina?" he asked.

"Yes." She felt her heart skip. "My family died," she added, still holding onto the lie.

"That's right. I was a senior in school." He chuckled. "God, life was simpler back then." She smiled slightly, wishing he'd change the subject.

She'd never been comfortable around cops, especially when she was lying about who she was.

Oh, she knew her license and information was good. The government had seen to it themselves, a fact that Crystal had assured her of years ago. She'd never asked how Sarah's mother had had the contacts to make things like that happen, and she doubted she wanted to know at this point.

"I asked you out a few times." His eyes met hers.

"Yes." She chuckled, hoping it would hide her nerves. "Things just never really worked out."

He nodded, then wrote something down in his book. "So you are seeing Mr. Carriveau?"

She was thrown for a loop once more. "How is this going to help find whoever broke into my room?" She leaned back.

His eyes moved up to hers and held there. She was thankful when another knock sounded on the office door.

"Come in," she called out quickly and was relieved when Adam walked in. Immediately he was on guard.

"What's happened?" he asked Carl.

Carl stood up and tucked his booklet into his pocket. "Just had a few more questions for Lilith." He turned and, as he was walking out, bumped shoulders with Adam.

"Excusez." Adam stepped further out of the way. "Oh." He stopped the man from exiting. "We have these."

Adam pulled out the notes from his pocket and handed them to the man, who frowned down at them.

"We've found three of them, but the first one is gone." Adam frowned at her. "But we've found these since then."

"I'll put them in the file and look into it." Carl tucked them into the folder and then said sternly to Adam, "I'll be in touch." Carl glanced back at Lilith then quickly disappeared out the door.

"What was that all about?" Adam turned to her and moved closer.

She shrugged. "I'm not quite sure. Apparently, he believes you're the one who trashed my room." She felt a shiver run down her entire body when she remembered that someone was still out there, stalking her.

Adam scowled at the door. "Pourquoi?" He turned to her and when he noticed that her eyebrows had moved up, he shook his head. "Sorry, it's an old habit. Why?"

"Beats the heck out of me." She frowned, then remembered why Adam was in her office. She jumped at the chance to get her mind off of the notes and the madman who wanted her. "Let's talk about Shane."

She leaned back slightly and watched his face change from anger to concern.

"I've already apologized to Shane and the other members of my staff." He sighed.

"Good." She crossed her hands.

"I don't appreciate my employees bad-mouthing you."

Her eyebrows shot up again. "I don't care what people say about me, employees or guests. We should never manhandle—"

"I get it," he broke in. She heard the remorse in his tone. "I'm sorry." He sighed, then stood up and walked around the desk. "I guess you could say I let my temper get the best of me." He laid his hands softly on her shoulder as he turned her chair towards him. Then he pulled her up until his arms wrapped around her.

"I'm sorry," he said into her hair.

"How am I supposed to stay mad at you?" she said into his shirt.

He chuckled. "You're not."

Finally, she pulled back. "So, are you set for tonight?"

He frowned down at her. "I was thinking…"

She shook her head after seeing determination in his eyes. "You are not backing out."

He frowned. "After what happened—"

"No." She crossed her arms over her chest. "I accidentally lock myself in a closet and you want to cancel everything." She almost stomped her foot but stopped herself.

"Lilly." He took her shoulders. "The wardrobe had been moved back to block the door. There is no lock on the door."

Somehow, his words skimmed over her mind.

"Don't be silly," she said. She felt her knees weaken, so she sat down.

"It's the truth. Come." He took her hand and pulled her up once more. She followed him silently to the attic, where the workers were back at work.

They walked over to the closet and she saw it for herself. It was an older handle without a spot for a key. She looked at both handles and shut the door, yanking it open again smoothly. Then she stepped back and tried hard to get the heavy door to swing shut on its own. It wouldn't budge. At least without a little help. She felt all the blood leave her face.

"Someone…"

"I'm staying." He broke into her thoughts. She turned to him and noticed several of the workers watching them.

"No," she said softly. "We need to finish this." She felt her anger grow. "I'm done being scared. Whoever is doing this needs to be caught and our plan will work," she said quietly. "Go, I've made sure everything is in order."

"But…"

"Adam, we may not have another chance at this when Sarah and Ben return. Then I'd live the rest of my life in fear like I used to." She started walking out of the room, and he followed her closely.

"Okay, but promise me you'll make sure to have your phone on you at all times until I get back tonight."

She nodded. "Of course. I only left it…" She shook her head. "Never mind. Yes, it won't happen again." She smiled.

They made a scene after lunch of kissing each other goodbye. Everyone knew each other's schedules, so it was no surprise that he climbed aboard as other employees got off the ferry.

They had checked the schedule themselves and noted who was coming and who was going. Only three people left on Mondays and four arrived. Two maids, one waiter, and Stacey, who worked at the main desk.

Plus, Rodney had requested the next two days off due to a doctor's appointment in Portland. His grandson was driving him down there. She didn't see a need for either of them for the next few days since the rain had hampered any work they had been scheduled to do.

She had leaned against the railing and watched the ferry slowly disappear.

"Your guy taking off on you?" Kaleen said as she stepped out and lit a cigarette then blew the smoke towards her.

"No, Adam's off shift for the next few days." She turned to go.

"Don't get any ideas about filling your free time with Tristen." The woman leaned on the railing and glanced off towards the ferry as it left in the rain.

Lilly barely held in a chuckle. "That won't be an issue." She turned and walked into the hallway.

"Miss Brown, there's a Marcus Stein on the phone for you," Marla, a young woman Sarah had hired over a year ago, said from behind the front desk.

"Thank you, Marla. I'll just take it in Sarah's office." She made her way up the grand front stairs.

She walked into Sarah's office, sat down, and picked up the phone. She didn't know who Marcus Stein was or what he wanted, but she figured it was another part of the daily life of running the resort.

"Hello?" She settled her breath from the rush up the stairs.

"Miss Brown?" The man sounded older and bored.

"Yes, this is Lilith Brown. How can I help you?"

"I know this may sound strange, but I'm wondering if you are a survivor of Hurricane Katrina?"

She felt the entire room spin as a hollow buzzing started in her ears.

"Miss?" The man's voice came again.

"I'm sorry, I think you have..." She was about to hang up.

"I understand if you're afraid. It's just, my client has hired me to track down her daughter."

She shook her head, closing her eyes to the tears that started falling and swallowing back the fear. "I... I'm sorry I can't help you."

"I understand. My client's husband died during Katrina," he continued, stopping her from hanging up.

"Dave? Dave died in Katrina?" She felt a wave of relief wash over her.

"Yes." He paused. "Miss Kincaid, your mother"—he sighed— "for the longest time had assumed you had died too. That was until a few days ago."

"I... how? Why?" She laid her head down on the cold wood, trying to breathe.

"She's a woman that loves to read the society magazines. There was a wonderful story of a recent marriage..." She heard some papers being shuffled. "A Benjamin Rothschild to a Miss Serenity Holley."

"Sarah," she corrected.

"Yes," he coughed. "Anyway, there was a large picture that went with the article. I believe you were the bridesmaid?"

She nodded her head, not trusting her voice. Then sighed when the line remained silent. "Yes," she supplied.

"Your mother knew instantly that it was you. That she'd found you, Cara Kincaid."

Adam stood under the awning and avoided the rain. He normally didn't mind a good summer storm, but this one was really starting to get on his nerves. He didn't like that his grand-mère had to drive in bad weather. Especially coming out to the docks to pick him up.

He watched her car pull around and stepped over to the driver side with the waiting umbrella.

"Why don't you get in, son, so I can take us into town for some dinner?" she said, reaching for the door.

"You know very well that I like to drive," he said in a soft tone, looking down at her.

"Oh, phooey." She barked with laughter. "You're just afraid of my driving." He helped her get out of the car and walked her around to the passenger door.

Sonya's French accent had retreated long before, leaving her with a very unique and colorful way of talking.

"Gran," he started to say, only to have her eyes narrow at him.

"Don't you Gran me." She turned to him once he sat behind the wheel. "You're up to something." She crossed her arms over her chest. "And don't think we're not going to discuss it over dinner." She turned back and stared out the front windshield. "When it rains this much, I like to eat at Roy's. A good greasy burger is called for." She glanced at him quickly. "If you're good, I might even throw in a chocolate shake." She chuckled at the face he made.

They drove the two miles into town and parked outside of Roy's, one of the only family diners in town that knew how to cook food good enough for his liking. He helped his gran out of the car and into the restaurant and as they sat down, he glanced around to see if he recognized anyone. The room was full of strangers. He'd only lived in Silver Cove for a few months, but his gran had moved here a few years back. Of course, she waved to everyone and chatted with them like they were old friends while he sat in silence and waited until things died down.

After placing their orders, she folded her arms on the table and just looked at him. He smiled back at her.

It had been almost eighteen years since he'd seen that face for the first time. There were a ton of new lines and wrinkles across her forehead, but there was also a heck of a lot more laugh lines around her eyes and mouth than when he'd first arrived.

"Spill," she finally said, her eyes narrowing.

"Tu es belle." He reached for her hands and pulled them up to his lips.

"Flattery will get you nowhere," she said, but he noticed her eyes soften. "What are you up to? Why do you need me to tell everyone you're staying in town when you're really heading back to the resort?"

He sighed, then leaned closer and lowered his voice. He spoke to her in French in a soft tone.

"Do you remember the woman I was telling you about, Lilly?" he asked, waiting for his gran to catch on.

"Of course," she said back in fluent French. "The girl you are smitten with?"

He chuckled. "Yes."

"What about her?"

"Someone has been stalking her. They have left some pretty crazy notes." He remembered the pieces of green paper he'd given to Carl.

She gasped. "That's terrible."

"I'm going back to the island tonight to stay with her," he added.

His gran smiled. "You're in love." It was more of a statement than a question.

"Yes." He smiled, then frowned. "I need to be there to protect her."

"Of course, you do." She leaned forward and patted his hand. "Go. Be safe though. I know you didn't like to be on the water during the storm—"

"I'll be fine," he broke in, just as their food arrived.

"Before you go," his gran said once the waitress left, "I have something for you at home."

He smiled. "You didn't have to give me anything but your love." He reached over and squeezed her hand. "And you've given me enough for a lifetime already."

She blushed, and he saw a tear come to her eyes. "You really are too much." She patted her hand over her heart. "Never an ounce of trouble. If you ask me"—she said in between bites— "your parents were just too selfish to raise you themselves." She looked up at him. "It's a good thing too because I don't know what I would have done if they hadn't sent you to me."

"I was a hellion," he added, frowning into his soup.

"You were a nine-year-old boy." She waited until he looked at her. "Nothing more."

He felt something in his chest shift. "Speaking of my parents, have you heard from them lately?"

His mémère frowned and set her fork down. "They are having problems," she said, looking down at her food.

"What kind of problems? Money?"

She laughed. "No. Marriage."

He frowned. "How bad?"

"Your mother is thinking of moving to the States."

"That bad?" She nodded.

"Your father…" She sighed. "I never liked the man. His head has always been too far into politics and chasing other women."

"Other women?"

"Yes, why do you think they moved you here?"

"Because I was a hellion."

She chuckled. "Yes, you were." She reached over and patted his cheek. "But it was so he could have time to pursue his desires."

"What about my mother?"

"She didn't want to raise a boy to follow in his footsteps." She frowned down at her plate and pushed the half-eaten burger away, disgusted.

CHAPTER 15

*L*illy floated through the rest of the evening shift. Her mind wasn't really on her work or even the conversations she'd had with guests or employees. By the time the evening meal was over, she was desperately wishing for a hot bath and a couple aspirin.

Even the weather had taken a turn for the worse again. More lightning lit up the night sky and thunder crashed loudly throughout the buildings. She dashed through the rain, along with several other employees, to their building and climbed up the stairs while Heather chatted with her about her day. She was only half-listening to her story.

"I'm sorry, I guess I have a headache," she said when Heather asked her a question that she hadn't heard. "I'm going to go in, take a bath, and relax for the night."

"Okay, if you need anything…" Heather added.

"Thanks." She unlocked her room, stepped in, flipped on the light, and screamed.

Then she sighed and closed her eyes until she heard

Heather pounding on her door. Quickly opening it, she smiled. "Sorry, saw a spider." She rolled her eyes. "Guess I'm going to hunt it down, then take a bath."

Heather took a step back and cringed. "I would help…"

"I know." She smiled. "Go, save yourself. Night." She shut the door and flipped the lock.

"You could have warned me," she hissed at Adam, who was reclining back on her bed as if he'd been there for hours. "Or turned on the light so I knew you were here already."

"So, I'm a spider, am I?" He chuckled.

"Heather has arachnophobia. I knew she wouldn't ask to come in if it was a spider." She walked over and pushed his booted feet off her still-clean bed.

"How did everything go?" he asked, sitting up.

"Fine." She walked over, tossed her shoes into the corner, and sat down in her chair, which was still holding her blankets and pillow.

"You?"

"Fine. I came back just before sunset. I didn't want to chance the weather getting worse." He paused when lightning lit up her room. "Which seems to have paid off."

She realized that he'd just risked his life to get back to her and she sighed. "I'm grateful you did. I was worried about you." She realized that was partly the cause of her headache. Now that she knew he was okay, the majority of it dissipated.

"You didn't have any problems?" he asked, moving to the end of the bed.

"No, everyone acted normal." She shrugged, thinking

about the phone call. "I…" She took a breath. "I do have something to tell you, but…"

"What?" Worry instantly crossed his face.

"I received a phone call today."

"From?" He leaned forward, reaching out and touching her knee. "Is everything okay?"

"A private detective. That my mother hired."

"Your… mother, mother?" he asked. When she nodded, he just stared at her blankly. "But, I thought…"

"Yeah, so did I. I just figured all these years that I got away because they were both…" She sighed. "It seems that Dave died in Katrina, but my mother, Carolina, survived." She felt a tear slide down her face. Adam was up instantly, pulling her into his arms.

"I'm sorry."

"No, don't be. She was never really there for me. She always took Dave's side and when I tried to tell her about… him, she blamed me."

"How did she find you?" he asked, pulling her down to the edge of the bed.

"Sarah and Ben's wedding photo in the papers."

"What does she want?" His hand was rubbing up and down her arm, removing the chill that had come over her.

"To talk." She shrugged. "I guess."

"The PI didn't say?"

Sighing, she admitted, "I guess there was too much buzzing in my head to hear anything more after he told me he knew who I was."

"Did you get his number?" Adam asked. She nodded and handed him the sticky note. "We can call him tomorrow." He tucked it into his pocket. "For now,"—he stood up— "I believe you mentioned something about a bath?"

She allowed him to walk her backward until her shoulders bumped up against the bathroom door. He fumbled as he reached behind her and opened the bathroom door.

They stumbled into the room together as he caught them and moved until she was once more pinned between him and a door.

"I've missed your lips," he said as his lips rushed over hers.

"You've only been gone for a few hours." She gasped when his teeth scraped up her neck, causing goosebumps to rise all over her skin.

"Too long," he growled next to her ear. His hands pushed her clothing away quickly, only moving away from her for a moment as he tossed his clothes aside.

When they were both naked, he pushed his body back up against hers and pinned her to the wall. His hands skimmed over her as his mouth nibbled every inch of her exposed skin.

She raked her nails along his back, needing to pull him closer to her as his mouth worked down her body. She'd never experienced the pleasure that spiked through her when his hot mouth found her soft folds.

Her fingers dug into his hair, holding him in place as his tongue lapped at her and she took her pleasure. Her shoulders pushed against the cool wood as she closed her eyes and silently begged him not to stop.

"Tell me how much you missed me," he said against her skin.

"Yes," she agreed. "More," she begged.

"More?" He chuckled. "Like this?" His finger dipped into her heat as his mouth continued its pleasure.

This time she screamed out his name as she felt her legs fold out from under her.

"Easy, I've got you." He lifted her up and walked her into her standup shower. "Your shower is bigger than mine." He frowned at the space. "And you have a seat." He shook his head.

Her mind was still too foggy to register his complaints, so she just moaned and nodded in agreement.

"Who did you have to kill to get this bathroom?" He pushed the shower head aside, so she wouldn't be shocked by the cold water and turned on the faucet. When the water had warmed, he flipped the showerhead towards her.

Just one more thing to like about him.

"Sarah," she said absentmindedly.

He chuckled. "Sarah is still alive." He lathered soap all over her skin.

"No, Sarah set it up for me. Since I don't go to the mainland, she gave me the room with the nicest bathroom. I actually had to wait a whole year to move in here."

The water was clearing her mind and she wondered about his pleasure. Glancing down at him, she realized he was still fully hard and ready to go, which only made her feel more on fire than before.

"Adam?" She moved closer to him, her hands roaming over his chest as he moaned slightly.

"Hmm?" he asked, his eyes going dark just before they closed.

"Does it work both ways?" she asked, softly.

"What?" He leaned his head back against the tile.

Instead of answering, she sat on the bench, taking his thighs into her hands and moving him a step until his hardness was right in front of her face.

"Lilly," he warned, just before she took him into her mouth. When he groaned with pleasure, matching her own sounds from moments ago, she realized it did work both ways.

She used her mouth on him, much like he had on her. Learning how to please him turned her on even more. This time it was him who screamed out her name.

His hands came under her arms, pulling her up. "As soon as I can think again, you are in so much trouble." He pulled her next to his body. "Where did you learn that?"

She giggled. "From you." She sighed as he pulled her hair under the water and started running his soapy hands down its length.

"I talked to my mémère today. She says my parents are getting a divorce."

She leaned back. "I'm sorry to hear it."

"Don't be. From the sounds of it, my father has been cheating since before the ink dried on the license. It sounds like my mother is going to be moving here."

She stood back and looked at him. "How do you feel about that?"

"Probably as excited as you feel about talking with your mother."

She laid her head down on his chest. "Promise me that if we ever have kids, we'll be better parents to them than they were to us." She felt him still, then sighed. "Sorry, it's been a long day." She started to pull away, but his arms around her stopped him.

"No, I like the sound of that." He put his fingers under her chin until she looked up at him. "I like thinking ahead to our future." He ran a kiss over her lips. "You are going to make an incredible mother." He smiled down at her and she felt her heart skip.

Adam lay in the bed, eyes wide open, staring at the ceiling and listening for the hint of any sounds. Every now and then, the room would light up from the storm, but the thunder was too far away now to wake Lilly up from her deep sleep beside him.

Her warm body was pressed against his, causing him a little discomfort, but he knew she was worth the sleepy limbs and tightness in his shorts.

His mind played over the day and he wondered how long they would have to wait until her stalker made his move.

He must have fallen asleep because a few hours later he awoke and heard the shower running and saw the light streaming through her window.

When Lilly walked out of the bathroom, wrapped in a towel, he smiled at her.

"Guess we had a peaceful night."

She nodded. "I hope you ended up getting some sleep."

He yawned, then nodded. "Since I'm not really here, I'm going to see if I can get a few more hours in after you leave."

She smiled. "I wish I could crawl back in there with you." She frowned as her eyes roamed over him. "I really, really wish I could."

"So, do," he coaxed.

She backed up a step and shook her head. "Can't. The men are supposed to start sealing the floor in the attic today. Plus, I have orders to place, invoices to scan, and…" She smiled. "A kitchen to oversee since my head chef is slacking off for the day."

He chuckled. "I did plan on doing some work too." He nodded to the computer he'd set on her desk last night when he'd snuck in.

"What kind of work?" she asked, pulling on a dark cream skirt.

"Just something I've been working on." He felt his face heat and tried to change the subject. "You look amazing this morning."

"What kind of something?" She didn't fall for the change of subject and crossed her arms over her chest, waiting. The fact that she was only wearing the skirt and her bra was a big turn on.

"I'm writing something," he supplied.

"What? Like a book?" she asked, pulling out a blouse.

"Sort of." He frowned and wished she'd move on.

"Really?" The excitement in her voice was intoxicating.

"It's nothing really, just a cookbook and a guide on how to grow your own spices and herbs." He shifted slightly in the bed.

"Why don't we grow our own on the island? I mean, there must be plenty of space." She started buttoning her blouse. "There's room between the back door and the employees' store." She turned back to him. "Could you get me a list of things you'd need? I can have Rodney get them once he gets back. Maybe we can even put up a little greenhouse, so you can grow year round."

The enthusiasm in her voice grew and he could see her excitement.

"I was meaning to ask Sarah once she returned. I felt it was too early to, before the wedding." He tucked his arm behind his head and watched her slip into a sexy pair of heels.

"Are you going to wear those for our date tonight?" he asked.

"Our…date?"

He smiled. "Forgot it already?" He made a tsking noise. "Our date night. You were going to wear that…"—he made a growling sound— "sexy dress for me."

He watched her eyes sparkle. "Yes, I remember. Don't you think it's a bad idea now? Considering… everything?"

"You let me worry about that." He got up from the bed and handed her the dress from the closet. "Just be up here in this, around eight."

She took the dress and smiled at him. "That I can do. What are you going to do about food? Should I bring up…"

"I came prepared." He nodded to his duffle bag. "Don't worry about me. Go about your normal day and make sure to keep your phone with you."

She walked over to him and placed a soft kiss on his lips. "I won't forget. Get some sleep. You look like you could use it."

She turned to go. "Lilly." She stopped and looked back at him. "Call him, find out what she wants, then call me on my cell." He handed her the card for the PI that she'd given him earlier.

She looked down at it, slowly nodded, then took it and walked out.

His body was demanding that he crawl back in between the sheets, but his mind was too busy. So, he pulled his laptop to the bed and lay down as he did a little research on Lilly's past.

Almost an hour later he found a report from the hurricane that listed all the lives lost and saw Cara Kincaid and David Kincaid listed with a surviving family member Caroline Kincaid. There were grainy pictures of the family, both parents smiling, while Lilly—Cara—stared at the camera as if she were already dead inside.

His eyes moved to the man who had tortured the young girl and he was thankful the man was already gone. He hated to think of what he would do if he wasn't.

Still, he was torn, knowing her mother had sat back and allowed the abuse to continue. He had encouraged Lilly to contact the woman because he knew she needed the closure. Just as the call he planned on making later today to his parents would be for him.

He read report after report and found out everything he could about the hurricane. After seeing pictures, he wondered how a teenage girl could have ever survived such wreckage alone.

When his eyes grew tired from reading, he shut his laptop down and closed them for a while. When he woke again, he showered, dressed, and then sat at her desk and worked on his project.

He liked the idea of raising his own herbs on the island and took the time to make up a list for Lilly along with some basic plans for small, simple greenhouses.

When his phone rang, he answered after seeing Lilly's name.

"How did it go?" he asked.

He heard her sniffle, then she sighed. "She wants to see me."

"Why?" He waited.

"She says she wants to apologize for the past. She sounded really happy that I was alive. She insisted that she'd changed. Even said she'd found God and had started going to church. That it was part of her new life, closing out her old one." He heard her chuckle. "Part of me wants to let her live the rest of her life letting it hang open."

He thought about the phone call he was going to make after he hung up with her. "Don't. You'll just suffer along with her."

It was silent for a while. "When did you get so smart?"

He smiled and then chuckled. "I've always been smart. Or so my mémère always says."

"When am I going to meet her?" Lilly asked.

"When Sarah and Ben come back we'll plan a dinner."

"I'd like that. Well, I have to go. I've got several things on my list that need to be done before our date tonight."

"Me too." He glanced down at the crockpot and enjoyed the warm smells coming from it. "See you soon."

After hanging up, he punched the number for his father first. That call didn't take long. He refused to yield on his feelings and let everything out in the open. His father listened to everything, then acted as if he was bored instead of hurting.

When he hung up with him, he felt that he had barely scratched the surface of his emotions. When his mother's phone rang, he held his breath and waited.

"H…hello?" She answered in English and sounded like she'd been crying.

"Mère?" He asked, "Are you okay?"

"Yes," she said again in English, which was strange

since he had never heard either of his parents speak English before.

"What's wrong?" he asked in English.

"I've just gotten back from filing divorce papers from your father," she blurted out, then broke into fits of crying.

He leaned back in the chair and realized he might run a little late for his dinner date.

By the time that Lilly returned to her room, she was nervous and excited at the same time. She'd changed into the dress in the bathroom at the end of her hallway, so no one would see her walk upstairs in an evening dress and ask her about it.

It was a lot harder sneaking into her room than she'd thought. She wondered how Adam had done it the night before. Then she remembered that he'd arrived before dinner had been over when half of the employees were busy with the meal.

When she opened her door, the smell hit her, and she felt her stomach growl.

Adam stood in front of her window, her desk pushed up against the wall, a white tablecloth covering it. Candlelight flooded the room with a soft glow.

Her desk was set like a table at a fine dining establishment, like their own dining room in the building next door. Two glasses of wine stood next to bowls full of what looked like chicken stew.

Soft music played from her radio, making the entire scene complete.

"How did you…?" She blinked, then turned and saw Adam for the first time when he stepped into the candlelight.

He wore dark suit pants and a jacket, with a crisp white shirt underneath. His hair was combed back, and he was freshly shaved. He looked like her mind's version of what James Bond would look like if he'd snuck into her room and cooked dinner for her.

"How did you do all this?" she asked, flipping the lock on the door behind her.

"You look amazing," he purred. For the first time, she realized that his eyes were glued to her. She'd almost forgotten that she was wearing the dress he liked.

Smiling, she did a slow turn and he gave a low whistle.

"Thank you." She moved closer. "I'm not sure how you managed to pull this off without leaving the room, but I'm impressed." She sat down when he pulled out the chair for her.

"It wasn't easy, but I think it turned out okay." He sat across from her. "Shall we see?" He held up his glass of wine and she took hers. "To getting rid of the old and starting new."

She smiled. "I like that." She clinked her glass to his and took a sip. "Mmm, the good stuff." She narrowed her eyes. "Which came from…"

He smiled. "My mémère's wine closet." He laughed.

She'd never really been on a date before. Once, when she'd first moved in with Sarah and her mother, Sarah had tried to take her on a blind date, but the evening had been a disaster, as the boy kept trying to grab her. Everything had been too fresh and raw from her past and she'd decided to never try dating again.

But with Adam, the rest of the evening passed beautifully. Not only was the meal wonderful, but the conversation had flowed so smoothly that by the time all the food was gone, she had forgotten her nerves.

He pulled her up from the chair, pushed it aside, and danced with her across her small space, kissing her slowly until she felt her entire body melt.

He pulled back and looked down at her. "I thought that we would enjoy a movie together."

She laughed. "Really? Because I was thinking…" Her hands pushed his jacket aside.

"Yes, that too, but… first things first. This is a date, yes?" He took his jacket off the rest of the way, then walked her over to the bed and let her sit down. He took one of her feet and slipped off her heel, slowly rubbing her foot until it relaxed. Then he repeated the process with her other foot as she moaned with pleasure. "Real dates include dinner, dancing, and entertainment."

"Weren't we on our way to… entertaining ourselves?" She smiled up at him.

He chuckled, then kicked his shoes off and climbed next to her, taking a moment to fluff the pillows behind her. Then he grabbed the TV remote and flipped on her set and DVD player.

"I have never seen this one before, but my mémère loves it."

He wrapped an arm around her shoulders and she leaned back into his chest as *Breakfast at Tiffany's* started playing.

She wanted to tell him this was her favorite classic

movie but decided against it and just sat back to enjoy the movie portion of her very first date.

The next morning, she woke up, stretched next to Adam, and wondered if her life could get any better than this.

Last night's date had ended like most girls were warned against letting first dates end. Slowly making passionate love to the man she loved was something she had only ever dreamed of doing.

Now, she couldn't imagine ending each evening any differently. She sighed and once again thought about spending the day in bed with Adam. Then she realized that the Robinson clan was due to disembark today. Glancing quickly at her window, she saw the hint of the sun coming up and realized that there wasn't a cloud in the sky.

Starting to sit up, she was held into place by a hand covering her breast.

"Hmm, I like this." He moved his palm slowly, making her giggle.

"Let go. I've got a million things to do today."

"Cancel them all and stay in bed with me," he said into her hair.

She pushed his hand aside and rolled out of bed. "Can't. Besides, there's too much…" She stopped dead when she noticed the green piece of paper by her door.

"What?" He was up in a second, glancing around. When he saw the note, he walked over and picked it up.

"You think this is a joke? I've been too nice. What happens next is your fault!"

"Son of a bitch!" He growled and stormed over to catch Lilly as she fell forward. He lifted her up and carried her back to the bed, stroking her hair and lightly calling her name until the color in her face returned.

"I…" She swallowed. "I thought he'd given up."

He blinked a few times. "Why would you think that?"

She looked up into his eyes. "I don't know. I guess I had hoped." He waited. "I thought it was Kaleen," she finally blurted out.

"Who's Kaleen?" She sat up with her back to the headboard and tucked the sheet around her as if she was chilled.

"Tristen's…"—she shook her head— "I guess she's his fiancée."

"Why would you think it was her and not him?" he asked, not trusting himself to touch her, to comfort her right now.

She glared at him. "I told you, it couldn't be Tristen. We had a talk."

"Right," he said sarcastically. "And, because of this talk, you know that it couldn't be him."

"Exactly." She crossed her arms over her chest.

"Okay, so why her then?" he asked.

She bit her bottom lip. "She said something to me the other day that made me think."

"What did she say?"

"Just that she was a very jealous woman." Again, he waited. "You know, the note said…"

"Yes, I see." He nodded and thought about it. "They're leaving the resort today?" She nodded. "I'm shadowing you all day until they go then," he demanded

"Like hell you are." She jerked herself off the bed and stormed to the bathroom, then turned back towards him. "If it is Kaleen, then all of this will stop when they leave. If it's not, you following me around like a… guard dog, won't help anything." She walked in and then shut the door behind her, leaving him no time to respond.

He sat and listened to her shower and came up with another plan.

When she came out of the shower, he walked over and wrapped her in his arms. "I'm sorry," he whispered into her hair. "This just has to stop." Pulling back, he looked down into her eyes as he pushed a strand of recently dried hair from her forehead. "I'm cutting my four days off short and will go back to work. Besides, sitting in your room the entire time, it's not exactly productive." He sighed.

"What about working on your book?" she asked.

He shrugged. "I can't concentrate knowing that someone out there is about to step up their game." He leaned down and kissed her. "Plus, I wanted to get started on the greenhouse. I figured I'd head into town and get some of the supplies I needed." He glanced out the window. "Looks like we're going to have a beautiful day to work outside."

"Rodney should be back sometime today, but if you want to start the work before talking to him, I have a corporate credit card you can put the supplies on. Come up to my office before you leave and you can put whatever you need on it."

"Wow, Sarah must really trust you to give you one of those," he joked, enjoying that he'd successfully taken the worry from her eyes.

She smiled. "We're sisters. Well, sorta." She frowned slightly.

"What?" he coaxed.

"It's just... I didn't tell her about the notes," she confessed.

"I thought you told her everything."

"Sure, about the break-in, being locked in the closet." Her eyes met his. "About us."

"Why didn't you tell her about the notes?"

"I didn't want her to worry." She walked over and started pulling on cream slacks and a dark mocha shirt. "Besides, if I'd told her, she would have been on the next flight home instead of snorkeling or jumping off cliffs."

He made a tsking noise.

"Oh, don't judge me." She turned and slipped on a pair of heels. "Now, if you're quite done, I'm going to be late." He chuckled. She walked over and stood by the door. "Do what you want. I have the card up in my office. You can swing by after breakfast." She turned and disappeared down the hallway.

It took him less than half an hour to sneak out of her room and head back to the dock where he'd tied up his boat behind one of the big yachts, where no one would dare look for it during the storm.

He made his way back to Silver Cove's docks and settled the small boat back into his slip. Then he waited for the morning ferry to the resort with the rest of the employees that made the daily trek.

"Are you heading back to work so soon?" Carmen, the head housekeeper asked him.

"I've got a new project I want to run by the... temporary boss lady." He smirked.

"That's not all I hear you're running by her," someone else joked.

He chuckled and ignored all the other comments that flew around as they made their way towards the island.

Jerry, the ferryman, wasn't present today. Instead, a different guy pulled up, causing the entire crowd to question where JT had gone.

"I'm Todd. Jerry asked me to fill in for him for about a week while he goes to LA to settle his movie deal." Everyone made noises.

The entire population of Silver Cove knew that Jerry, aka JT Whistler, was one of the most popular science fiction writers of the century.

"Which book?" someone shouted out.

"I don't know anything more," the new man said. "He'll be gone for about a week and he said to give out my number in case of emergencies." He handed everyone a small piece of paper with his number on it.

Adam tucked it into his pocket along with the latest threatening note.

When the ferry docked, he made his way up to Lilly's office and knocked.

"Come in," she called out in a very professional voice. When he pushed the door open, he watched a wave of relief wash over her.

"Hi." He coughed and walked in. "I have a new proposition to run by you," he said loudly, then shut the door behind him. Her head tilted, and her eyebrows shot up. "Sorry, too many ears in the hallway." He winked as he walked over and kissed her solidly on the lips. "I missed you," he whispered to her.

"Ditto." She smiled up at him. "I have the credit card." She handed him the plastic.

"Did you know that Jerry is gone for a week?" he asked.

"Yes, he's gone to LA to start the movie project for *Crescent Creek*."

He snapped his fingers. "Won that bet," he joked.

"What bet?"

"Nothing, just a few of us on the ferry ride over were making wagers on which book would be made into a movie first." He smiled. "I guessed right."

She smiled. "Is there any question? I mean, all of his books are amazing, but *Crescent Creek*." She shook her head. "It gave my goosebumps goose bumps," she joked. "Have you stopped off in the kitchen yet?"

"No, I will on my way out. Actually, I was going to see if I could enlist someone to help out today, seeing as the big group is leaving soon and we only have a smaller group coming in."

She nodded. "I think we can spare a few people if you need more help."

"No, just one. I was thinking of taking Rob."

She leaned closer to him. "I think he and Heather are…"

His chuckle stopped her. "Yes, they are."

Her eyebrows spiked up. "How do you…" She shook her head. "Never mind. I don't want to know. Go, get what you need, just as long as you stay within this budget." She handed him a printed piece of paper of the list he'd emailed to her yesterday.

"I'll try," he joked, then he walked over and gave her another kiss that had his entire body shaking with desire.

"Go," she said hoarsely, "before someone walks in."

"Would it be such a bad thing?" He sighed, then took a step back. "Will I see you for dinner?"

"I'm counting on it." She smiled as he walked out.

*A*fter Adam left, it took her almost ten minutes to get her mind back in gear. She sat around daydreaming about making love to him on Sarah's desk. Which did nothing to help her get the stack of orders placed. She shook her head clear and tackled her work.

She was finding the job easier and easier as time went by. Managing the employees was the hardest task, but since she and Adam were now getting along, things were going very smoothly.

By lunchtime, she felt like she'd jinxed herself. An hour before the Robinsons and other guests were scheduled to disembark, she found two of the housemaids actually fighting in the hallway.

The women were pulling each other's hair and there were red scratch marks down one of their faces, while the other had a fat and bloody lip.

She quickly pulled the two young women into her office and took the next fifteen minutes to listen to them explain that they were sisters and one of them had cheated with the other's boyfriend.

In the end, Lilith threatened to fire them both if they couldn't keep their private lives out of the guest quarters. Both women swore they could control themselves, and Lilith gave them a week off without pay to settle their differences.

She walked downstairs to make sure that the Robinsons were happily on their way and almost bumped into Tristen, whose hands came up to her shoulders to steady her.

"Sorry," she mumbled and took a step backward, only to be irritated when he moved with her and kept his hands on her.

"I was hoping we'd bump into one another," he said in a low tone. "I know we're heading out soon, but I wanted to thank you for everything you did for my family."

She smiled politely. "I'm just doing my job. I'm happy we could accommodate your family."

He took a step closer. "I know I asked before, but I was hoping you'd change your mind. If you're ever in New York…"

Her chin came up. "Thank you, but I'm seeing—"

"Yes, I understand, but that doesn't mean you can't come visit for some fun." He rubbed his hand up her arm.

She quickly stepped back, breaking the contact. "I appreciate the offer, but…"

She heard a high-pitched growl, then felt the wind knocked out of her as she was pushed forward violently.

A body slammed into her, causing her to fall on all fours as her hair was ripped backward, causing her neck to jerk back.

"You bitch!" she heard Kaleen growl in her hear.

As soon as it happened, the woman was yanked off of her. Lilith glanced around and saw Tristen holding Kaleen back. The woman's perfectly groomed hair was flying everyone as she spat and kicked at him.

"You bastard. I told you to stay away from that bitch!" she hissed as she scratched at him.

Lilith got up from the ground and assessed the damage. Her slacks were ruined on both knees. She was bleeding slightly from her left knee and felt a pinch in her neck when she tried to turn.

"What the hell?" someone said from down the hallway. "Are you okay, Kaleen? Take your hands off of her." The woman rushed forward.

"She attacked Lilith," Tristen supplied. "I'm not letting her go until she calms down." He held onto the woman tighter.

"Remove your hands now, young man, or I shall call your family into this matter," the woman snapped at him. At this point, Kaleen had calmed down and was just glaring at her.

Lilith took a step back when Tristen's arms dropped.

"I want this woman fired," Kaleen barked out.

"You're lucky if she doesn't sue your family and get every dime of your trust fund," Tristen added, crossing his arms over his chest.

"What's going on?" Someone else joined the mix. "Oh, you're bleeding." Tristen's mother rushed to her side. "Oh, you poor girl. Did you fall?"

"Kaleen attacked her. We were just talking. I was telling Miss Brown how much I appreciate all she's done for our family's stay and psycho here rushed over and attacked her from behind."

Kaleen turned and glared at Tristen, then moved towards him. His eyebrows shot up. "Go ahead, why don't you tell your mother what else you've been up to." He nodded towards Lilith.

"I don't know what you mean." She glared at him and crossed her own arms.

"Locking Lilith in the attic? I saw you coming out of the attic." He turned to her. "I swear I didn't know you were in there, locked in the closet, otherwise I would have helped. But I put two and two together after they found you."

She nodded, rubbing her hands together to try and relieve the ache.

"I don't know what you're talking about?" Kaleen glared at Tristen even more. She turned to her mother. "I was at dinner with you. Remember? I couldn't have locked her in a closet or anywhere for that matter." She turned to Lilith and glared.

"I know what I saw," Tristen said. He nodded to Kaleen. "I saw you leaving that room"—he nodded towards the attic door a few feet away— "after dinner the night Lilith went missing."

Everyone turned to Kaleen. The woman looked around the group, then growled. "Fine, I went in there to talk to her, to tell her to stay away from you." She shrugged. "I saw her go into the closet and I shut the door behind her." She smiled. "No biggie. I mean, she could have left at any time."

"Someone moved the wardrobe in front of the door," Lilith said softly.

Everyone turned back to Kaleen, who glanced around, then rolled her eyes. "Okay fine, I might have nudged the thing back."

Kaleen's mother turned immediately to Lilith. "I'm so sorry for all the trouble my daughter has caused you."

Kaleen snorted. "Don't apologize to that… maid. She's nothing." Kaleen's eyes ran over her. "I mean, just look at her. What are those? Knock off Dolce & Gabbana's?" She chuckled.

"They were, yes," Lilith said proudly, then glanced down at the ruined slacks. "Ones that I spent a whole week's salary on." She glared at the woman.

Kaleen waved her away. "Mother will cut you a check." Her mother's chin dropped slightly. Kaleen turned to walk away, then stopped. "Tristen, are you coming? I'm bored with all this." She waved around the group.

He laughed and shook his head. "Not on my life." He turned to his mother. "I don't care how much you think it would benefit the family, I won't pair myself with this"—his eyes moved over Kaleen— "woman. It wouldn't do anything but harm the Robinson name."

"I quite agree with you," his mother added. "Now, I think we should help…" She looked towards her.

"Lilith." She supplied her name again.

"I think we should help Lilith clean up. Don't you?" She turned to her son, who nodded. "I wouldn't be surprised if you hear from Miss Brown's lawyer," she added as they walked down the hallway towards Sarah's office. Lilith looked back and saw Kaleen's mother grip her by the arm and pull her back into their room.

She walked in and hobbled over to sit behind the desk.

"I'm okay. Really." She pulled out some napkins and dabbed at her leg through her ruined pants.

"Nonsense. I insist we call a doctor here to have him look at you." Tristen's mother moved to pick up the phone.

"No, really. I'm fine. I'll just run to my room and clean myself up and change." She stood up.

Tristen's mother put a hand on her arm. "I was wrong about you," she said softly. Then she sighed. "It appears I was wrong about a lot of things." She glanced towards the door. "If you want, I know the name of several very thorough lawyers."

"That won't be necessary." She sighed, then turned to Tristen. "Do you know anything about Kaleen writing me notes?"

He'd been leaning against the doorjamb of the office but stood up straight now. "Notes? What kind of notes?" He frowned.

"Threatening ones." She shivered remembering the one from this morning.

He shook his head slowly. "No, but I can ask." Before she could say anything more, he had disappeared down the hallway.

"Someone's been threatening you?" Mrs. Robinson sat down across from her. "What on earth for?"

She shrugged. "I thought it was because she was jealous that Tristen was showing me attention."

"Tristen shows a lot of women attention." His mother waved the comment away.

She shrugged. "So I gather," she said dryly.

A few minutes later, Tristen came back in. "Unless she's lying, she had nothing to do with any notes you've found."

Lilith felt her stomach roll. She'd been hoping they had solved everything. Well, except the initial break-in to her room, since that had happened before the Robinson's had arrived at the resort.

"Thank you," she said, standing up. "If you'll excuse me, I'll just go and clean up now."

Her knees were started to swell, and her wrists and neck were hurting more and more. She planned to swallow several aspirins before heading back to work.

"If you need anything…" Tristen's mother added. Then she turned to her son. "Come, we still have some packing to do."

They left the office, and Lilith rested her head back against the chair. Suddenly she was very tired and wished Sarah was around. She would know how to handle this.

After a moment, she got up and made her way slowly towards her room. Sitting on the edge of her tub, she peeled off her ruined clothes and dabbed some peroxide on the cuts. Then she lathered on some Neosporin. It took a few bandages to cover the cuts and she doubted she would be able to bend her knees without most of them falling off. She downed an aspirin and looked at herself in the mirror.

Her hair was a mess, her shirt had blood on it, and she looked like she'd just had a night with no sleep. It took her a few more minutes to freshen up to where she looked halfway decent.

She pulled on another pair of slacks, this time a pair from Sarah's old clothes, and a crisp white blouse and slipped on flats instead of the heels she'd been wearing earlier. She doubted she could take the double pain of heels with her knees swollen and bruised.

When she walked out, she bumped solidly into Adam.

"Someone said they saw you come up here." His eyes moved over her, then he was pulling her into the room quickly. "What's wrong?"

"It's…" She shook her head, feeling the tears that she'd been holding in break loose. He held her until the crying stopped.

"It was Kaleen. She locked me in the attic" she said between sobs. "She didn't leave the notes or break in to my room, but she locked me in there and…" She leaned back. "She attacked me."

She felt Adam tense. "She attacked you? When?"

"About half an hour ago. She pushed me down and…" He took her hands and cursed under his breath when he saw the raw marks.

"Where else?" he said, slowly touching her. When his hand rubbed on the outside of her slacks, she moaned softly.

"Both knees are pretty bad." He reached to remove her slacks. "No, later. I have to…"

"To hell with work," he growled and started gently removing her pants.

"Adam." She took his hands. "I'm okay. I guess I just let it build up." She closed her eyes. "I'm better now."

He waited until she moved her hands then slowly pulled her pants down her legs, removing each shoe as he went. When her bruised and skinned knees were exposed, he gasped softly.

"Have you seen a doctor?" he asked, rubbing his fingers gently around the red marks.

"No, I'm fine, really. I used to scrape my legs up worse than this."

"Why did she do this?" he asked, looking up at her.

"I guess she was jealous and a little crazy," she added with a chuckle.

"Have you called the police?"

She blinked. "No, of course not."

"Lilly," he started but she stopped him.

"Her family, the Bauers, may not be as powerful as the Robinsons but they are pretty damn close. If I did call them and they hauled her into jail, she would be out before they could even fingerprint her." She shook her head. "There's no reason."

"The woman has to pay for what she's done."

"From the look in her mother's eyes as she followed her daughter down the stairs, I guarantee Kaleen will pay."

Adam watched Lilly walk back into the main building and cursed once more under his breath. He'd done everything he could to try and talk her into taking the rest of the day off, but she was too stubborn, something he'd instantly liked about her but now was finding quite annoying.

She'd talked him out of marching into the building and handling the situation with Kaleen's family himself. His temper was still spiked, so he chose to expend the energy plowing up the land and digging the posts for his new greenhouse.

The materials wouldn't be delivered until early next week, but he figured he could at least get most of the hard work out of the way now, especially since he had the time and energy.

The sun had come back out full force and he'd even had to remove his shirt as he worked. He watched the

Robinson clan depart and glared towards Kaleen. She was being dragged behind what he could only assume were her parents.

The docks sat empty now and he knew that most of the new guests wouldn't arrive for a few more hours, allowing the resort employees plenty of time to turn over the rooms and clean the place from top to bottom.

When he'd finally worked off most of the anger, he went in and showered off, then went to find Lilly before the dinner break.

He found her up in the attic. The room had turned out better than even he could have imagined. The floors shined with the new polyurethane coat.

"Aren't you supposed to stay off this for a few days?" he asked from the doorway.

She turned and shook her head, smiling.

"They said twenty-four hours. It's been close to thirty." She waved him in. "Isn't it perfect?" She spun around slowly. He could see that her knees bothered her, so he moved to her side and took her in his arms.

"I'll wait until tomorrow to move the furniture in." She smiled. "The bar will go over there." She nodded towards the wall with the closet on it. "That way the wait staff can bring the food out through the closet." He felt her shiver. "Then we'll have tables lined up around the entire room and leave the middle open for dancing." She sighed. "I can just imagine our first wedding party up here." She glanced around the room dreamily.

"I think Sarah will be impressed with what you've done."

She turned to him, wrapping her arms around his shoulders. "I hope so. I was watching you work outside."

Her eyes moved down to his chest. "All sweaty with your shirt off." He watched her tongue slowly move over her bottom lip and felt himself grow hard with desire.

"And?" His eyes were glued to those sexy lips of hers.

"And I can't believe how much it turned me on to watch you with a shovel."

He smiled. "Not as much as it's turning me on knowing you liked it." His hands slowly made circles across her back as she pressed herself closer to him.

"I was thinking…" She bit her bottom lip and he released a low growl.

"About?" It came out as a whisper.

"Us on a hardwood surface." She smiled and took his hand, then slowly started walking towards the door.

"Wait," he stopped her. "What's wrong with this surface?"

She smiled and shook her head. "I was thinking more like the desk in Sarah's office."

He felt his body begin to boil. Taking her hand, they quickly made their way towards the office. He pulled her in and pushed her up against the door, claiming her mouth in a searing kiss that shook him to the soles of his shoes.

His hands pulled and tugged her clothing off and she let out a soft cry as he tried to tug her slacks down her legs. He'd forgotten about her bruises and cuts.

Slowly, he dropped to his knees and gently removed her slacks, then kissed each knee.

"Adam." She pulled on him until he was pushing against her again. "Don't slow down," she muttered then gasped when his fingers found her.

"No," he growled, "this will be anything but slow."

He was right—the speed matched that of his desire for

her. His fingers were tangled in her hair, holding her mouth to his as he laid claim to her. Her body reacted with each touch, each nip of his teeth on her skin.

Only when he felt himself on the edge did he allow himself to slow down. His hands stilled against her skin, his lips covered hers as he enjoyed the taste of her.

"Come for me, Lilly," he said against her lips. "I'll follow you," he promised.

"Adam, I…" She pushed herself tighter against him, her eyes closed tightly as his fingers found her softness, then she was exploding around him. She threw her head back and he'd never seen a more beautiful sight. Moments later, he followed her and held onto her like his life depended on it.

CHAPTER 18

The next two days were, even more, a blur to Lilith than before. It wasn't that she was particularly busy, but she did spend a lot of time setting up the attic and organizing the bar area. She'd found everything she needed for the space in the boxes that had been stored in the attic.

She even found several large paintings that now hung in the space. She'd ordered the tablecloths and had to replace several tables and over a dozen chairs, which had been hard to find.

Already, she had a party booked for the space in two weeks. She'd had a photographer come and take pictures, so she could update the resort's website. After she surprised Sarah, of course.

Everything had fallen into place nicely.

She'd even stopped receiving the notes and was even more sure it had been Kaleen than before.

Less than two days after the Robinsons and Bauers left,

she received a certified notice from the Bauer's lawyer with a check attached.

She'd been shocked to see so many zeros. Adam had insisted she think about everything before signing the paperwork and cashing the check. She'd promised to wait until Sarah returned before making her decision.

Her knees had healed up nicely, but she still had bruises. She covered them up by wearing slacks, which bothered her since the weather had turned very warm after all that rain they had gotten.

The day before Sarah and Ben were set to return was the busiest day so far. She spent most of the day in the office, making sure everything was perfect. All of the invoices were scanned and filed, and all of the orders were up-to-date.

Her evenings were filled with Adam. They had taken to spending their nights in her room since it was almost double the size of his and the bigger shower had come in extra handy.

Every member of the staff knew they were together. They also knew about Rob and Heather, who seemed to have a rockier relationship since Rob was always complaining about how Heather was complaining. Still, they were very cute together when they were acting happy.

The next morning, Lilly stood on the front porch and watched the ferry arrive. She twisted her fingers enough that Adam reached up and took her hands in his.

"Stop, everything's going to be fine," he whispered to her.

"What if she doesn't like—"

"Stop. They're going to love it. Besides, from the

sounds of it, you already have it booked up for several occasions."

She smiled and relaxed. "Three." She watched the couple walk slowly up the sidewalk, holding hands.

"They look happy," he said, squeezing her hand lightly.

They did. Both of them were a little tanner than before. Ben's hair had grown out a little during the trip to where it was borderline shaggy. Sarah looked amazing. She was wearing an off-the-shoulder flowered sundress and heeled sandals. Her hair was pulled in a braid off to the side and there was a bright pink flower above her left ear.

When they noticed her, Sarah dropped Ben's hand and rushed to give her a hug.

"I missed you," Sarah whispered.

"Me too." A tear slid down her cheek. "Mrs. Rothschild." She giggled. "So." She leaned back and cleared her throat. "I have a late wedding gift for you." She smiled.

"Lilith, you shouldn't…"

She held up her hand, stopping her friend. "If you'll follow me." She turned to Ben who was shaking Adam's hand. "Both of you." He frowned slightly, but then took Sarah's hand in his.

"Lead the way." He motioned.

She walked in and stood aside in the hallway, which was filled with employees, who were all cheering and clapping.

"Welcome home," everyone chortled at the same time.

"Thank you," Sarah said once everything quieted down. "I'm sure we will have plenty of time to catch up with one another over the next few days, but until then…

Get back to work," she said playfully, as everyone laughed.

"Thank you." She turned to Lilith.

"Oh, no. That wasn't your surprise." She smiled and took her friend's hand, then led her up the main staircase and didn't stop until they reached the attic doorway.

"What—?" Sarah started to say.

"Close your eyes." Lilith waited until Sarah and Ben complied.

Lilith took Sarah's hand and pulled her into the doorway. She didn't stop until they stood in the middle of the room. Glancing around, she noticed that everything was perfect.

"Okay." She took a deep breath and waited.

First Sarah gasped, then Ben. Lilith watched as Sarah did several spins, her hands covering her mouth as her eyes grew wet with tears. "It's just like I remember it."

Lilith was taken back. "Remember?"

She turned to her. "Yes, when I was a child." She watched her friend's tears slide down her cheeks. "I remember dancing with my father up here. Before he got sick. Then…" Ben walked over and wrapped his arms around her. "Then, my father died, and they moved all the storage up here." She turned to Lilith. "You did all this?"

"Me and the extra money you found in the budget last month." She smiled, then Sarah's arms were around her, holding her tight.

"Thank you. It's perfect."

"It's already booking out too," Adam added from the doorway.

Sarah turned to him, then back to Lilith. "Really?"

She nodded and smiled. "Three events so far."

"Sounds like you made a good choice making her manager," Ben added.

"Temporary manager," Lilith added.

Sarah looked at her and winced. "Actually…" She took her shoulders. "I've got a surprise for you."

"Manager!" Lilly said for the tenth time.

"Yes, I heard." He chuckled. She stopped on the pathway leading to the employee quarters that evening.

"But, manager." She stretched the word out and smiled over at him.

"Yes, I also remember her saying you had the next week off." He smiled. "And, she was nice enough to allow me two more days since I spent two day's building that." He nodded towards the beautiful greenhouse he'd built with the help of Rodney and his grandson. "So, I was thinking…" He stopped under the light just outside the doorway. "What about spending some time on the mainland. I did promise you a boat trip."

She wrapped her arms around him and smiled. "That sounds nice."

The next morning, they set off on the ferry, both weighted down with a bag. They were surprised to see Jerry manning the helm.

"I thought you were going to be gone a lot longer?" Lilly said, rushing up the stairs to give the man a hug.

"Naw, just a few days to sign all the paperwork. The real long trip comes this fall. They want to set me up in an apartment for six months for filming."

"Six months in LA?" Adam broke in, his arm going around Lilly's shoulders.

"Yeah, it's going to be tough being away from here so long." Jerry looked out to the water and sighed. "She's my mistress."

Lilly smiled. "Still, six months while they make your book into a movie. Who are they going to get to play the lead?"

Adam leaned against the railing as the two of them went through a list of actors and characters for his movie. Some he knew, others he didn't. When the ferry docked, they disembarked, and he could feel Lilly's nerves kick in.

"Hey, she's going to love you." He took her hand and pulled it up to his lips to kiss.

"I've never met someone's family before," she said, causing his eyebrows to shoot up. "Other than Sarah's."

He chuckled. "If you can handle Crystal, then my mémère will be easy." He tugged on her arm until they stopped in front of the car.

"Grand-mère, this is Lilly. Lilly, my gran, Sonya."

Lilly held out a hand to shake, but then his mémère surprised even him by walking over and wrapping her arms around Lilly.

"It's a pleasure to finally meet you. I've heard lots about you from Crystal." She winked at her. "I take one of her yoga classes, silver sneakers." She smiled, her chin rising slightly. "I'm the oldest one in the class." She leaned closer and whispered. "And the most limber one too."

"Gran," he warned, rolling his eyes. "Remember, not in front of me," he said in French.

"English, boy. It's rude to speak a different language in front of our guest." She slapped his arm playfully. "Why don't you put those bags in the trunk while I walk with Lilly." She turned to Lilly. "I thought we'd walk over to Ed's for some pizza. Then we can head to the docks for our evening boat trip." Sonya wrapped her arms through Lilly's as they started walking and talking.

Adam piled the bags in the trunk and followed them two blocks to Ed's.

He'd never laughed so hard having lunch with Mémère before. Even though she managed to embarrass him more than he'd ever been, he enjoyed every minute of it.

After they ate pizza, he was surprised to learn that Mémère had packed his favorite dishes for the next day and a half in a large basket and cooler.

"Mémère, how did you get all of this in the trunk?" he asked as he was unloading it from the car at the docks.

"I asked the neighbor boy to help." She patted him on his cheek. "Adam worries about me too much." She took Lilly's arm and started walking towards his boat.

"This is yours?" Lilly asked when they stopped in front of his 36-foot boat.

"Sure, I had big plans for her." He smiled and tossed his bag over and then set the cooler and basket down. Next, he held out his hand to help Mémère in first, then Lilly. "Welcome aboard." He kissed them both.

"It's for luck," Mémère said, smiling. "My père used to do the same." She walked over and sat down. "Come, sit. Adam will get everything ready."

Lilly looked around the boat as she made her way to sit on the soft bench.

"I'm impressed," she told him once she sat down.

"What? Did you think it would be smaller?"

"Well, yes." She laughed. "For some reason, when you

mentioned you had been stuck out in a storm... I guess I pictured the boat from *Gilligan's Island*." She laughed.

"From?" He turned to her and frowned. "What is... *Gilligan's Island*?"

She laughed and shook her head. "A classic show that we are going to seriously have to catch you up on."

He took the next few minutes getting the food and supplies downstairs. Just as they were about to leave, mémère stood up and sighed. "Well, this is where I leave you two."

"Leave?" Adam frowned. "But you're coming with us."

"No." She patted him on the cheek. "This is a trip for you two." She leaned close. "I've packed a little something special for you in my bag." She winked. "Go, have fun, be young." She leaned up and kissed him on the cheek. "Besides, I don't want to miss any of my yoga classes." She turned to Lilly. "It was a pleasure to finally meet you. I know we'll have plenty of time to get to know one another soon."

"Are you sure you don't want to come?" Lilly asked.

"Oui." She smiled. "Aller avec le vent," she said, then he helped her out.

"Sorry, once she makes up her mind about something..." He sighed as he watched her walk back to her car alone.

"I think it's charming that she set this up so we can have the time to ourselves." Lilly leaned back and rested against the seat.

"You think that's what she had planned all along?" He turned to her. "To not go?"

"Why not." She shrugged.

He thought about it as he untethered the boat, then sat down and turned the boat engine over. "Well, I was going to stick close, because of..." He glanced back as the car pulled out of the parking lot. "But, if you're up for it, there's this secluded beach a little further down the coast."

She waved her arm. "You're the captain."

He chuckled and pulled out of the docks slowly. When they hit the open water, he gunned it and a smile spread on Lilly's lips. She'd tied her hair back, but still, strands of it found their way loose. He motioned for her to join him up in the copilot seat. She held onto the back of the seat and made her way forward to sit next to him.

"Would you like to take the helm?" he asked. She quickly smiled and nodded. He moved over and let her take the wheel, then stood beside her as she leaned her head back and laughed.

"I love the wind." She laughed, throwing her head back and smiling over at him.

He knew at that exact moment that he would do anything to please her just like this for the rest of his life.

CHAPTER 19

They traveled south for almost an hour before he took the helm again and slowed the engine down.

"Wow, what a rush." She smiled as she straightened her hair. "I never imagined it would be so much fun."

"I remember the first time I went out onto the water." He sighed, and his eyes became dreamy. "I was scared to death and excited all at the same time."

"How old were you?" she asked, settling into the seat next to him.

"Five." He glanced at her. "My grand-père was a captain, remember?" She nodded. "He wanted his son to follow in his footsteps."

"And?" she asked when he went silent.

"He had a daughter instead." He chuckled.

"Right." She nodded.

"So, naturally, he wanted his grandson to have sea legs." He maneuvered the boat closer to the shoreline.

"What happened?"

"I got seasick." He chuckled. "Terribly. I had to be hospitalized for a week with an inner ear infection."

"Oh, poor child." She reached out and took his hand.

"It took me ten more years to get back on a boat. Mémère took me out again. She's always had a boat. Even when she moved here and married her second husband." He leaned closer. "He was an investment banker."

"What happened to him?"

"She's outlived both of her husbands." He sighed. "After that, she was determined to live alone. That was until I came along." He smiled over at her and she could see the love in his eyes.

"I never knew my grandparents." She added, "I guess I never knew my real father's family at all. I suppose I could have cousins out there." She thought about it, then shrugged. "If so, I never knew about them."

He reached across and took her hand. "There's still time to learn more about them."

She turned and looked at him. "I'm not sure I want to know more about them. I mean, they had plenty of opportunities to reach out to me." She thought about it, thought about the conversation she'd had with her mother's PI. "Besides, I've decided not to get in touch with my mother."

"Why?" he asked, slowing the engine down.

"I have all the family I want here." She smiled, thinking about Sarah, Crystal, and the people she'd surrounded herself with over the last thirteen years. People who had helped a teenager start fresh, even though they knew she was running and hiding from something.

Adam squeezed her hand, then raised it up and brushed a kiss across her knuckles. Then he released her hand and focused on steering them to a small rocky area and cut the engines. "Can you help me tie up?" He turned to her.

"Um, sure." She bit her lip, concerned she was going to mess something up.

"It's pretty easy. All you have to do is toss this rope to me once I get over there." He picked up a rope and nodded towards a pile of rocks.

"How——?" she started to ask, but then realized they were drifting towards the rocks still. Then she gasped when she realized just how fast they were approaching the dark wall of rocks.

"I've got it," Adam said, standing on the edge of the boat, then glancing over at her. "Ready?" He handed her the rope.

She nodded since she was too afraid to speak. He used his legs to stop the boat from slamming into the rocks, then when they were moving backward, jumped easily across the space and landed on the flat rock edge.

"Now," he called out to her, holding his arms out. Without thinking, she tossed the rope across the space and squealed when he easily caught it.

He planted his legs wide and when the boat started drifting too far, gave the rope a gentle nudge and had it once more drifting towards the rocks.

Images of crashing into the sharp edges flashed through her mind.

"Easy," he said, just before he once more made sure the hull didn't smash into the rocks. "I'm tying us off." He rushed over to a large rock and then she noticed the small piece of metal that had been hammered into the massive side.

"It's called a cleat," he called out. "See?" He swung

the rope around it several times. "Easy." He turned back to her and she felt the boat settle. "Now comes the hard part."

Her eyebrows shot up. "That wasn't hard?"

He chuckled. "No, the hard part is carting everything for our picnic down to the beach." He nodded towards the left and she glanced over to see the sandy spot. It looked completely untouched.

"Wow." She moved to that side of the boat and watched the water splash up on the soft sand. "How did you find this place?"

She hadn't heard him come back on board, but his arm rested around her. "What do you think I do on my days off?"

She glanced up at him. "Well, according to the stories you used to tell Rob, you had a line of women you used to get busy with." She smirked. "Rob's words, not mine."

He chuckled. "Stories. How else did you expect me to win their respect?"

She thought about it, then smiled. "With Rob and a few others, I guess you're right."

He turned her towards him. "Short of winning you over, that is." He leaned down and rubbed his lips across hers. "Now, that we're together, I've gotten more respect than before."

"That just proves that you should have been nice to me from the start."

He smiled. "But seeing you riled up was way too much fun."

She couldn't help but laugh.

Adam spent the next half an hour setting up their picnic. He dragged the small folding table and chairs down to the sand, then carried the cooler and basket of food.

It took him several minutes to convince Lilly to enjoy the beach, instead of helping him. He'd helped her onto the rocks, then handed over her bag. She'd settled on a towel in the sand and kept watching him. He could tell she wanted to help, but he was determined to make everything perfect for the evening himself.

He went back to get some candles he kept in the cabin and noticed his grand-mère's bag. Walking over, he flipped it open.

She'd packed him a nice teal button-up shirt and caramel-colored cotton pants. He glanced at himself in the mirror and frowned. He did look rather rough. Deciding quickly, he pulled them out, only to have a small box fall at his feet.

Reaching down, he picked it up, then flipped it open. Inside sat his grand-mère's wedding ring from her first marriage. She must have told him the story of the ring a hundred times when he was younger.

The ring itself was a marvel to look at. The fact that it still shined as if new didn't surprise him. Instead, it was the shape of the ring that had him twisting it in the light. He'd always loved how the gold twisted into a flower shape with tiny diamonds covering the petals and a larger one held in the middle. The band even had a few leaves twisted into it.

The story of the ring and how it had been hidden and saved during a time of war was the real gem. The fact that it was still in his family was nothing short of a miracle.

Glancing down, he noticed the note tucked in the

bottom of the bag. His grand-mère's handwriting had grown a little sketchy over the years. Still, she'd written the note in French, which meant it was for his eyes only.

"You know what to do with this. I'm so proud of you and happy you've finally found your happiness and your heart. – With all my love."

It took him only a few minutes to change and he was shocked when he walked back down to the beach to find she'd changed out of her shorts into a flowing white dress. She'd tied her hair up on top of her head as strands of it flowed around her face.

She was standing near the table, watching him. Walking over, he set the candlesticks and candles down, then gathered her into his arms.

"You look amazing." He smiled just before he kissed her.

"So, do you, and all of this." She nodded towards the table.

"There are just a few more things." He set up the candles and lit them then held her chair out for her to sit down. When she did, it quickly sank in the soft sand, causing her to laugh.

He finished setting out the food and then sat down in his own chair, sinking slightly into the sand himself.

"This all looks amazing." She smiled.

"I owe my love of cooking to mémère." He sighed. "I know everything is going to be perfect."

All throughout dinner, he felt his stomach roll with nerves. He'd never imagined asking a woman to marry him after only knowing her for six months, let alone dating her for less than two weeks. But there was no doubt in his mind that Lilly was his happiness and heart, as his mémère had put it.

He could no longer imagine his life without the woman sitting across from him. He only hoped she felt the same way. He waited until after they had eaten. The sun was just sliding down over the land, leaving the sky rich with bright colors.

He stood up, reached out his hand for hers, and helped her stand. "Walk with me?" he murmured.

She nodded and followed him to the shoreline. The beach was small, which only allowed for a short walk, and when they reached the water's edge, he stopped so they wouldn't get wet.

He'd been thinking about the words to say all evening. He knew he had one chance at this and didn't want to screw anything up.

"Lilly." He pulled her closer after placing a kiss on her soft lips. Then he stepped back and went down on one knee since in this matter, he was a traditionalist. He pulled the small box from his pocket and opened the lid slowly. "I've never met another woman who has stolen my heart so quickly. I can't imagine a life without waking up next to you, seeing you smile, hearing your laughter..." He saw a tear slip down her cheek as her hand went to cover her mouth. "There's only one thing that could possibly give me more joy than I feel when I'm with you, and that's if you'll agree to marry me and let me spend the rest of my life next to you."

He held his breath as he searched her eyes. When she pulled her hand away from her mouth, he saw the smile and felt the relief flood in.

"Adam, I've never met someone like you before.

Someone who could irritate me and make me want to kiss you at the same time." Her smile grew bigger and she chuckled. "I'd love to spend the rest of my life torn between the two." She nodded her head and squealed when he rose up and quickly hugged her until he felt his arms shake. When he stepped back, he removed the ring from the case and took her hand.

"This has been in my grand-mère's family for generations." He smiled. "And she wanted you to have it."

He heard her gasp, then saw more tears slide down her face.

"It's beautiful." She held her hand out in the dying light and then rushed back into his arms.

He'd never been as happy as he was then. They spent a few more moments watching the sunset, then she helped him gather everything up and take it back up to the boat. He set everything on the deck, then took her hand and a large blanket and led her back to the soft sand.

"Since it's still warm, I'd like to lay under the stars with you for a while."

"I'd love that," she hummed.

He laid the blanket out and heard her sigh when she'd finally settled in his arms. He held on to her for a moment, looking up into the night sky, dreaming of how wonderful their life was going to be.

When he felt her shift, he wrapped his arms around her and enjoyed the kisses she rained over his face and neck. His hands roamed up her legs, which had wrapped around his hips until he felt her shift once more. This time when she pressed her core to him, it was his turn to groan.

"Lilly," he growled next to her heated skin.

"Adam." She pulled back an inch. "Make love to me, here, under the stars."

Looking into her eyes, he realized he couldn't deny her anything. His hands went higher, cupping her softness until he heard her moan, then they were rolling until he had her shoulders pinned on the soft sand. Her skirt was hiked up to her waist, exposing her to his view. His eyes roamed over her body. He'd never felt so hungry for her, ever. He was starving for her touch, for her taste, to feel her body wrapped around his.

Her nails dug into him, then she quickly unbuttoned his shirt and pushed it off his shoulders. Her nails scraped his skin, sending more desire flooding through him. He'd never experienced this much desire.

When he slid into her, it was like coming home. They both moaned through a kiss that seared him more than he could ever have dreamed. His heart shattered into a million pieces, shooting stardust towards her.

They lay there, their breaths matched as they stared up at the stars, wrapped around one another until the air turned chilly. Then he carried her towards the boat and easily hopped the gap with her in his arms. She gasped, then giggled when he landed safely.

"I've never had a more perfect day." She sighed into his shoulder.

"There's plenty more where this one came from." He smiled. "And you've promised to spend them with me." He looked down at her.

"Yes, I have." She smiled up at him. "Take me to bed," she purred.

"As you wish," he agreed and complied.

CHAPTER 20

The next morning, Lilly was happier than she'd ever been. It started with breakfast in bed, then a cool dip in the water with Adam before they spent the morning on the small beach collecting seashells. They decided to eat lunch on the boat as they made their way slowly back to Silver Cove. They agreed to eat dinner in town since they were running low on supplies.

When they pulled his boat back into its slip, his grandmother was already there. He'd texted her and asked if she would like to join them for a celebration dinner.

When they walked off the dock, hand in hand, she rushed towards them and engulfed them both in a hug.

"Félicitations à vous," she said over and over. "Je suis tellement heureuse pour vous."

Lilly smiled, and replied in French, "Je vous remercie," making his grandmother smile even more.

"I told you she was the one," she said as she slapped Adam's cheek softly. "Now, let's get some food. I'm in the mood for pizza." She winked.

The pizza and the company were amazing. Just what she needed to end her day. When the last slice was finished, she heard her phone buzz.

"It's Sarah," she said, then answered the phone. She could barely hear her friend, so she motioned to Adam and his grandmother and stepped outside the door so she could hear better.

"Hey, I hate to bother you, but…"

"It's no bother, what's up?"

"Never mind. I can figure—"

"Sarah," she warned. "What?"

"I can't seem to find the orders for tomorrow." She sighed. "I've checked everywhere. I held off calling you until…"

"They're in the folder on your desk." She smiled.

"No, they're not." She sighed. "I swear, I'm gone for two weeks and it's like I forgot how to do anything," her friend growled. "Yesterday, I actually almost forgot to run payroll."

Lilly laughed. "Breathe. I'm almost done here, I can—"

"Nope," Sarah said, stopping her.

"I'll be heading back there anyway tonight."

"What? You still have until tomorrow."

Lilly looked in the window at Adam and his grandmother and smiled. "Yes, but I have some news I wanted to share with you. Besides, Adam will be staying at his grandmother's place and I feel kind of weird about staying there too."

"Have you talked to him?" Sarah asked.

"Not yet, but I'll tell him you had an emergency and needed my help."

"Don't use me as an excuse," Sarah warned.

"I'm not." She chuckled. "Trust me, I've had a wonderful time, I just need… some time to myself for a night." She sighed

"Okay, I could sure use your help. I'm drowning in paperwork here." She could hear Sarah shuffling paperwork.

"Oh, I forgot to tell you how to scan the invoices," she added.

"Scan?" Sarah asked.

"I'll show you when I get there, it'll save you so much time. I'll be there soon." She hung up before Sarah could respond and then walked back into the pizza parlor with a smile.

"Everything okay?" Adam said as she sat down.

"Yes, I'm going to head back to the resort. Sarah needs some help finding some stuff." She rolled her eyes. "Sounds like the honeymoon fizzled her brain."

Adam chuckled. "We can leave—"

"No." She reached out and took his hand. "You don't have to be back until tomorrow evening. Why don't you take some time with your grandmother?"

Adam glanced at his grandmother, who just smiled. "I do have a few things that I wanted to talk to you about." Lilly saw a slight frown cross the woman's face. Adam's face matched hers as worry crossed his eyes. Then he turned back to her. "I'll take you to the dock." He started to get up.

"No, I can find my way." She leaned up and kissed his cheek, then turned to his grandmother. "Thank you," she said and held out her hand, showing off the ring. "It's more beautiful than anything I've ever seen."

The older woman smiled and she was sure she saw a tear form in her eyes. Leaning down, she placed a kiss on the woman's wrinkled cheek.

She headed out towards the docks, her overnight back slung over her shoulder. So much was running through her mind with everything that had happened in the last few weeks. She'd never imagined being engaged. She glanced down at the ring on her finger and smiled bigger.

It was beautiful. Amazingly so. She'd never seen a ring like it. Its old-time charm was something she would have never picked for herself, yet it seemed to fit her personality perfectly. She couldn't wait to show it to Sarah and everyone else.

Her heart flipped every time she remembered seeing Adam fall to his knee. Her heart had almost burst with love when he's spoken those words to her. She'd known instantly her answer. She'd never been surer of anything in her life.

By the time she reached the dock, she felt like she was almost floating on air. Not only was she going to be manager of East Haven Resorts, she was going to be married to Adam. Married.

She'd texted Jerry to come pick her up but still ended up waiting a few minutes. When the boat approached her, she frowned as it pulled up next to the dock.

Adam helped his grand-mère out of the car and frowned when he saw another car parked in the driveway.

"I didn't know you had company." He frowned as he

turned towards her, then frowned, even more, when he saw the look in her eyes.

"I… I didn't know she would be here so soon." She blinked a few times and Adam felt his heart drop. He wasn't prepared to see his mother yet.

Then he glanced back towards the car and thought about heading out, meeting Lilly at the dock, running away back to the resort with her to escape what was sure to happen next.

"Adam." His grandmother's hand rested on his arm, stopping him. "Please, just listen to her. She deserves a second chance." She took a deep breath. "She's my daughter and even though I know she's been a complete idiot with most of her life choices, I, as her mother, couldn't turn her away any more than I could turn you away so many years ago."

He closed his eyes and felt pain and hurt swell from all the years of neglect from the woman standing in the window, watching them.

She looked older than he remembered, even though he'd only seen her just last year. Her eyes were filled with worry as they looked at him through the glass, waiting for him to make a move.

He turned back to his grand-mère. "Did you plan for Lilly to return to the resort?" He saw the answer in her eyes.

"I thought it would be best if she wasn't here for this. Not yet anyway. So, I called and asked if they would ask her to come back."

"You could have told me." He shook his head.

"No, you wouldn't have come back." She tapped his cheek. "You're too stubborn, like me."

He chuckled. "You're right." He held out his arm and waited until she wrapped hers in his. "Let's deal with this together." They started walking towards the house and he could have sworn he saw relief cross his mother's face.

When he stepped in, the room was silent for almost a full minute.

"I didn't think you'd come in," she said in English.

"I almost didn't." He looked down at his grandmother, who quickly patted his hand and walked from the room.

His mother walked over and sat down on the sofa. That was when he noticed she was wearing a pair of jeans and one of his old sweatshirts. He'd never seen his mother in anything but designer clothes. He was so taken back by it that it took a moment to understand she'd been talking.

"I'm sorry?" He shook his head and walked over to sit across from her.

"I'm sorry," she said, shaking her head. "I'm not as fluent in English as I used to be."

He nodded, prompting her to continue.

"I know we talked about what has happened. But I wanted to tell you the truth." She was twisting her hands in her lap. Her eyes were focused on his shirt, rather than his eyes. "That your father, he's the one that had affairs." He waited. "He's the one that filed for divorce."

"I thought you did?"

"No, he has, and he has plans to marry again." Her chin rose, and her eyes met his.

"I see." He felt his blood turn hot. "Why?"

"Why?" she asked, her head tilting slightly. "From what I know, she is pregnant."

He heard a light buzzing in his head. "I see."

"At first, I believed she was blackmailing him, but

now…" She shook her head and closed her eyes. "They have been together for a while."

"And?" He waited.

"Your father…" Her eyes moved back to his. "He is a very powerful man." She bit her lip and he watched a tear slide down her face. "He was just starting his career when you were born." She looked away. "Someone in his position, he needed to focus." Her eyes moved down to her hands. "I was nothing more than a showpiece and there was no room on his shelf for a son who was rambunctious."

"Then why have me in the first place?" he drawled.

"It was my choice." She avoided his eyes. "I wanted half a dozen children." She sighed and leaned back, resting against the sofa, a move he'd never dreamed he'd see his mother make. She looked relaxed, at home almost. "From the moment you were born, I loved you." Her eyes met his now. "I would have done anything for you. But then…" She closed her eyes again. "Charles, he wasn't having it, not after the party." She met his eyes.

"What party?"

"The party we held for his campaign. You were supposed to be upstairs, asleep. But, instead of falling asleep, you broke into his study and took his paperwork and made…"

"Paper airplanes." He closed his eyes and remembered watching each carefully crafted paper airplane sail off the balcony, raining down on the heads of the large gathering below. He'd released more than a dozen of them before his father had snatched him up. He remembered hearing laughter and feeling like he'd lightened the dull party up.

But the next week he'd been packed up and hustled onto a plane towards America to live with his grand-mère.

"Oui," she nodded. "That was just the last time. You had interrupted several meetings of his…" She paused, her eyes looking more tired now.

He could remember running into his father's office on multiple occasions. Sometimes he'd begged for his father to play with him, other times he'd been trying to escape the nanny. He'd even hidden in one of his father's cupboards during a meeting, then had been caught when he'd fallen asleep and had started snoring.

"I was nine," he growled out.

"Oui and your father had no patience for you."

"What's he going to do with the new kid? Ship him off too?"

"No." She looked down and a tear slipped down her cheek. "Apparently now he is ready to start a family. He's already released a press release."

"But…" He sat up. "Your divorce…"

"Was finalized two days ago in the tribunal de grande by his avocat. His reach in the court is pretty high up. I wasn't aware that the property was only in his name, which means… I have no title to any of it." Her eyes met his. "I've been left"—her chin rose— "with little more than the clothes on my back. It appears that now, I am the one he wishes to sweep under the rug."

He felt anger so strong he almost vibrated with it.

"What does your lawyer say?" He stood up and walked towards the window to look out at the dark sky.

"I couldn't afford one," she responded softly. "I was removed from the house, without any jewelry or clothing." She closed her eyes and this time, more tears streamed down her face. "Like a maid who had been caught stealing."

"We'll go public with this," he growled out. "He can't do that to you." He turned and walked over to her, gathered her up in his arms. "I don't care what you've done to me in the past, no one deserves to be treated like this after almost thirty years of marriage."

His mother almost collapsed into his arms. "I don't care about any of it. My only wish is to get back the time he took away from us." She leaned back. "I would have never let you go." More tears streamed down her face and she reached up with a shaky hand. "You were my most prized possession." She smiled. "You were the thing I wanted the most in life." She leaned up and placed a kiss on his cheek. "I should have fought harder for you."

This time it was his eyes that were wet as he wrapped his arms around his mother and held onto the first woman he'd ever loved.

CHAPTER 21

"Mother, why don't you come in here and join us," his mother said in French, smiling up at him.

He turned around and saw his grand-mère walk into the room, wiping tears from her eyes.

"Why don't we go into the kitchen and enjoy the crème brûlée I made earlier?" his mother added.

They were just walking into the kitchen when his cell phone rang. Seeing the number for the resort, he picked up.

"This is Adam," he answered.

"Adam, it's Sarah. Is Lilith still there with you?"

"No." He frowned as he glanced down at his watch. "She should be there already. Have you talked with Jerry yet? He might be running slow."

"Jerry never picked her up. He's at the dock now and she's not there."

Instantly his entire body was on alert. "I'm heading to the dock now." He hung up and rushed from the room.

"Adam?" his mother called out. "What is it?"

He turned, his eyes meeting his grand-mère's. "Lilly never made it to the dock."

"We're coming with you," his grand-mère shocked him by saying.

"Is Lilly—?" His mother started to say, only to have his grand-mère pat her arm.

"Oui." She gathered her purse and both women followed him out.

He drove double the speed limit and pulled up in front of the docks in less than five minutes. Jerry was there, on the phone, pacing the landing. When they pulled in, he glanced over and frowned.

"Anything?" he called out, holding the phone away from him.

"No." He scanned the road and cursed at the darkness. Even with the streetlights on, the road leading to the pizza place was dark.

"I'm heading up the block and looking closer," he called out. Since his mother and grandmother were already out of the car, he told them to wait there and took off on foot.

His mind raced over images of her laying in the gutter, bleeding. But when he reached Ed's Pizzeria, there was still no sign of her. He opened the door and glanced around, wishing he knew more people in town.

When he spotted Sarah's mother, Crystal, sitting with a younger woman, he rushed over to her. "Have you seen Lilly?" he interrupted their dinner.

"No." Crystal frowned at him. "Why?" Just then her cell phone rang. Glancing down, she answered it. "Hi, yes," She looked up at him. "Adam is here now. No," she answered, then stood up. "I'll help." She hung up and looked down at her friend. "I'm sorry, Karen, we'll need to reschedule. My daughter is missing." She took his arm and rushed out of the room.

"Where did you see her last?" she asked once they were outside.

"Right here." He pointed to the ground. "My grand-mère and I were sitting in there." He pointed to the table by the window. "She got a call from Sarah and…" He took a deep breath. "I wanted to walk her to the docks."

Crystal laid a hand on his arm. "It's okay, everything will be fine." She patted his arm. "Then what?"

He shook his head. "She started walking towards the docks."

Just then Crystal waved and called out to someone. "Joseph." She waved the man over. Even out of his uniform, Adam recognized him as one of the town's police officers. "Have you seen Lilith Brown in the last…" She glanced at him.

"Half an hour," he supplied.

She relayed the info to Joseph, who called back as he crossed the street. "No, why?"

"Seems she missed the ferry to the resort. She got lost somewhere between here and the dock."

The man frowned and glanced down the street. "Who was the last one to see her?"

"I was," he broke in. "My grandmother and I had dinner with her here." He nodded to the pizza place. "Could this have anything to do with the threatening notes she was receiving?" he asked, fearing the worse, but needing to know what the man thought.

"What notes?" He turned towards him, giving him all of his attention.

"The notes I gave your partner. He put them in her file when he came out to discuss her case."

Joseph shook his head. "I don't understand, what file? We haven't had time to look into anything but the initial break-in with the wine, which you solved for us."

He looked between the pair. "But he came out to the island." He frowned. "He asked Lilly more questions. I gave him the notes we'd found."

"I'm sorry." Joseph shook his head. "I don't know anything about that. Why don't we head down to the station and we can ask Carl ourselves?"

There was something she was supposed to do. Her mind refused to focus. Her fingers itched like she'd been playing a game of tug of war and had lost grip of the rope in her hands.

Her mind was too foggy to register the fact that she was swaying. The gentle rock of Adam's boat had lulled her to sleep the night before, wrapped in his arms. Reaching out now, she felt for him but came up short when her hands refused to move. She tried again, but this time her eye snapped open when she realized that her hands were tied together.

When she tried to sit up, she was held down. This time her eyes found the rope that crossed her chest. Suddenly, the swaying of the boat caused panic to rush through her.

She started screaming and kicking out, only to have the

door yank open on the small cabin as Carl walked in, smiling down at her.

"Good, you're awake. Now you can see your new home." He walked over and took her hands. She jerked back and tried to scoot away from him as tears slid down her face.

"Where am I?" she asked. Her throat felt raw and sore.

"Home." He smiled. "We're home now." He reached down and easily lifted her up into his arms as she fought him. "Hey!" He growled and squeezed her tight until she stopped fighting. "That's no way to act after I saved you."

"Saved me?" she gasped.

"Sure." He shook his head as he carried her up small stairs out onto the deck of a small boat. "You had just lost your way a little." He glanced down at her. "That Frenchman messed with your mind." He chuckled. "But now that you're home, everything will be normal." He moved slightly and nodded towards a row of lights.

From what she could tell, they were at the base of a bluff. An old dock led up to a small house buried in a thick forest of trees. It was too dark to tell, but she was sure there wasn't another building or road nearby.

"Where are we?" she asked again, still catching her breath from when he'd squeezed her chest.

"I told you"—he shook his head— "we're home." He started walking up the dock, towards the lights. This time, she kicked and fought harder, causing him to lose his grip. She hit the dock with a thud, losing her breath again, banging the back of her head hard against a plank of wood.

"Stop it!" he shouted at her. "There's no reason for you to fight. I've told you, you're home now." He growled out as he tried to gather her once more in his arms.

When she didn't stop, he reached back, and she felt his knuckles connect with her jaw, just before everything went dark.

The next time she woke, she was lying on a soft cot in a dim room lit by a simple gas lamp.

"I didn't have enough time to prepare your room like you'd like it." He glanced around. "But I thought you'd understand since you moved up the schedule some." He twisted around and flipped a pocketknife open. He was still wearing his uniform, his gun tucked and locked into his belt. Her eyes ran over the gun and pepper spray, which were locked into place with simple buttons.

Could she get to them in time? Should she try? So many questions ran through her mind.

"Why am I here?" She tried to remember what had happened to her on the dock but couldn't. Her mind was too fuzzy.

He stopped what he was doing and chuckled. "This is where you belong." He rolled his eyes like she'd just simply forgotten that she was supposed to be here.

"Is this your home?" she asked when her hands broke free.

"No!" he growled out and wrapped his hands around her raw wrists, causing her to gasp in pain. "This is *our* home." He looked around the sparsely decorated room. "Just like I promised you all those years ago."

She shook her head. "You promised?" He shook her shoulders and then dropped her back onto the cot. Her legs were still tied together, forcing her to realize she couldn't run for it just yet.

"Sure." He turned and smiled down at her. "When you showed up here, you got off the bus, broken and confused.

I made you a promise then, when I first saw you, that I would keep you from harm." He looked around. "I'm sorry it took so long. I had to get things ready for you."

She glanced around and felt her skin crawl. The place was a dump. There was no carpet on the floors, just exposed wood planks that ran the length of the one-room place. The fact that the lights were lit with gas instead of electricity made her question if there was electricity to the house.

"You…" She took a breath, thinking. "You built this place?"

He smiled. "With my own two hands." She watched his shoulders straighten. "Just for us." He walked around. "Of course, there's still a lot to do." He waved his hand around and began talking about things he had planned. She barely listened as her eyes scanned the dim room, looking for an escape.

There were only two windows, which appeared to be boarded up from the outside, and the one door, which he was currently blocking. Not to mention that her legs were still tied together. She knew that it was a long run down to the dock and what she could only assume was the only boat available.

Her options were not looking good. She felt herself shiver with fear.

"Are you cold?" he asked, taking a step towards her.

"Yes," she agreed. "I'm sorry." She shivered again, trying to control the shakes.

"I'll start a fire." He rushed across the room to a large stone fireplace. A pile of wood sat next to it, giving her an idea. All she had to do was play along with his delusions. It was the only way she saw to survive until Adam could come for her. First things first, she moved her hands behind her back and removed the ring from her finger, making a point to shove it on her other hand.

She doubted Carl would understand or allow her to keep it if he knew that she and Adam were engaged.

She remembered all the games her stepdad had played with her and knew exactly what she needed to do. Taking a deep breath, she readied herself for the game.

"If you untie my feet, I can help you make a fire," she said in a polite voice.

He glanced over his shoulder and frowned at her. "It's the man's job to start a fire," he said, leaning over the kindling and striking a match.

"Well, how about I boil us some water or heat up something to eat?" she said, trying to sound positive.

"No, I'll take care of you tonight. Besides, I think I gave you too much morphine." He shook his head. "I should have double-checked. It was wrong of me." He growled and then stopped when the fire took hold. Standing up, he turned towards her, a huge smile on his lips and his eyes sparkling like he'd just won the lottery. "Now, what would you like? Chicken noodle or tomato soup?"

$\mathcal{A}$dam stood impatiently waiting as Joseph talked to his captain about Lilly's case. When he was done speaking, the duo walked over to where he and Crystal stood.

"I'm sorry, Mr. Carriveau, Joseph has explained your situation." He shook his head and smiled over at Crystal. "Hi, Crystal."

"Hi, Tom." Her smile didn't reach her eyes and Adam could see the worry had tripled since he'd pulled her from the pizzeria.

"I'm sorry, there's not a lot we can do. If Carl was working on a file, he didn't tell anyone else about it."

"Is that normal?" Adam broke in.

"Well, it's not *not* normal." Tom chuckled.

"What about Lilly? Can you put out the word to look for her?" Adam questioned, feeling his patience slipping.

"I can have my guys keep an eye out for her, but there isn't a lot to go on. Like, if someone saw her being shoved into a car, or if someone saw her being attacked?"

"My god!" Crystal almost screamed. "Tom, this is my daughter we're talking about. Do something!"

He turned on her and gave her a look as if to say, 'Calm down.'

"Don't look at me like that. I took that girl in when she was thirteen. She's mine." Her eyes narrowed, and her small frame seemed to grow a few more inches.

"I'll put the word out to my cars. I've got a few out right now."

"What about Carl?" Adam asked.

"Carl?" Tom walked over and looked at the board. "Carl got off duty about an hour ago."

Adam looked over at Crystal. "Right when Lilly went missing."

"Hey now," Tom said, "I don't like where you're taking this. My guys are all—"

"Where's his desk?" he barked out to Joseph.

"There, next to mine." He pointed, following Adam.

"You work with the guy." He turned when he noticed that the desk was spotless. "Anything off about him?"

"Lots." He rolled his eyes. "The chief wouldn't hear any of it since we were short staffed, and Carl was home-grown."

Adam glanced over at him in question.

"Born and raised in Silver Cove," Joseph supplied.

"What are we looking for?" Crystal asked as Adam opened the drawers. He stopped dead at the last drawer.

"What?" she asked, moving closer.

There, in the bottom drawer, was a stack of green papers. With shaky hands, Adam reached in and took the top one.

. . .

"She's mine. Forever!"

He turned to Joseph. "Where?" he barked out.

"He lives a few miles from town." He rushed out, Adam quickly on his heels. "I'll drive," he called out then stopped. "Chief, don't put out an APB on her. He'll be listening."

Tom nodded his head and Adam noticed then that the old man's face had gone a little pale. Crystal walked over and wrapped her arms around the older man trying to comfort him.

"I knew his old man. I promised to look out for him after he was gone," he was saying as he and Joseph ran out the door.

"I trained the son of a bitch myself," Joseph growled out as he drove through town with his lights on.

"Why would he take her?" Adam asked a million questions in his mind.

"What did the notes say?" Joseph asked.

Adam filled him in as they hit the outskirts of the town.

"Sounds like he's delusional. I read about it a few years back." Joseph sighed. "Should have seen it myself. The man was always making up shit." He slowed down near the end of a drive. "You'll stay put until I come back for you." He parked the car and turned off all the lights.

"Like hell, I will," he growled out and got out of the car with Joseph, who just sighed.

"Listen, we don't know if he's brought her here or not. If so, he's armed with this." He waved the gun he'd drawn. "And possibly the shotgun from his trunk."

"Then give me one of yours," Adam said plainly. "I've

spent enough time at the gun range to handle either of them."

"You're not trained in situations like this," Joseph started to say.

"And you are?" Adam questioned, causing the man to halt.

"Fine, but we go in together."

"Of course." He nodded, then walked around and took the shotgun he was handed.

"Don't shoot. I mean it. You're only there to back me up," Joseph warned.

"Fine," he said, knowing full well he would break that promise if it meant saving Lilly.

Adam followed Joseph up the long drive. The sky was full of clouds that blocked out the starlight and the light from the moon, making the trek slow and troublesome. He stumbled too many times to count and grew more frustrated as they went along.

Finally, he could see a dim light come from a small building.

"I've only been here once, but there's a back door. I'll knock on the front door, you go around to the back and don't make a move until you hear me. Got it?" Joseph relayed.

"Sure," he agreed, then moved around the building, keeping as low as he could. He found the back door and started to move slowly towards it, just as the bottom of the door burst open and a large black dog rushed towards him.

He braced his feet, ready for the impact that never came. Instead, the dog stopped a foot from him and sat down in the dirt. Adam watched with amazement as the dog's tail wagged a million miles an hour, clearing the spot underneath its tail.

He could have sworn there was a grin on the dog's face as its tongue lapped the air around him.

"Hi," he said. He was surprised when the dog barked in reply.

"He's not here," Joseph called out, causing Adam to jump and spin around.

"How do you know?"

"He left the door open. I had a look inside. Roscoe," he said, getting the attention of the dog, "where's Carl?"

Roscoe barked and took off through the trees. "Follow him," Joseph called out, taking off.

Adam raced after the black spot as it weaved through the darkness, afraid he'd lose the dog and Lilly forever. His breath hitched, and his entire body ached as he forced himself to speed up. He lost sight of the dog only once and stopped to listen. When he heard the panting straight ahead, he sped up and almost stumbled into a clearing.

"There," Joseph called out. "There's a light." He pointed to a small speck in the distance. The building was no more than a shack hanging on the side of a bluff surrounded by trees. If it hadn't been for Roscoe racing towards it, he would have overlooked the spot.

Then, while they were watching, he saw the light grow stronger. His mind whirled as he raced towards the growing brightness. By the time he was a few feet from the door, the entire building was engulfed in flames. Joseph was close on his heels and he was reaching out his hand for the doorknob when the building shifted, and he was blown backward through the air.

The wind was knocked from his lungs and he hit a few

tree branches as he flew through the air. He finally landed on the ground with a thud. Then the darkness overtook him, and his mind cried out for Lilly and the future they would never have together.

Lilly waited and watched Carl work on making the soup on an old propane stove. She decided against trying to talk to him after the last time. She'd asked him how long it had taken to build the shack and had almost gotten slapped in response.

His moods were growing odder and she was afraid he was building up to something. He started mumbling to himself as he cooked. Every time his back was to her, she would scoot closer to the fire. If he asked, she would say she was just trying to get warmer.

She had to be a few steps in front of him. That was the only way she was going to get out of this alive.

"I've practiced this," Carl said over and over again. She noticed that he had started swaying slightly.

"What?" she asked, inching towards the fire.

"This!" he barked out and turned towards her. She released her breath when he didn't say anything about her being closer to the fire. "Us!" He set the bowl of soup on the table. "Being with a woman." His eyes narrowed. "I told myself I had to wait for you. Forced myself to wait." He grunted. "You're the only one." He moved closer to her. "The only one I'll be with. You're perfect. Just like I said you would be."

He was a foot from her. She could see the bulge in his pants and felt her stomach roll. Then he stopped. "But first"—he glanced back— "food." He nodded. "Yes, that's how it goes. Food first, then…" His smile grew, and she knew she wouldn't be able to ever smell tomato soup again without thinking of this moment.

He turned to go back towards the table and she jumped, her legs still tied together. She hit the gas lamp, knocking it from the small table. It landed just outside the fireplace, causing Carl to spin around and jump.

Oil splattered over the wood planks, as she reached for a piece of glass that had broken. She cut her hands on it as she swiped at the rope. He rushed towards her and yanked her arms back, but he was too late. The fire had leapt from the hearth and had now engulfed the oily planks of the floor.

Her feet were still tied together, but she swiped out with the broken glass and felt the skin on his face give way to the sharpness.

He holed out in pain as blood splattered over her shirt and face. His hands dropped away from her, causing her to lose her balance and fall forward only feet away from the growing fire. She rolled away, tucking her arms as she rolled over the broken glass from the oil lamp.

When she stopped, she reached down and continued cutting her rope, only to be yanked once more from behind. This time, when she kicked out, the rope broke free from her legs and she connected with his shin. He cried out in pain. She felt the butt of his gun jamb into her ribs. Closing her eyes, she counted and waited for death as the fire lapped around them, growing stronger and stronger.

Then, the pressure of his gun disappeared, and she was tossed forward. Pain shot up her arms as she connected with the panes of the window. The glass broke under her fingers, cutting her.

She heard Carl cry out and when she glanced back, noticed that the other oil lamp had burst next to him and he was completely engulfed in flames. He stopped for a moment, and his eyes traveled down to his feet where the propane tank sat, surrounded by fire. Then he looked up at her.

"Run!" he shouted just before a bright light flashed before her eyes, sending her flying out the barricaded window. She heard bones snap, felt skin break open, and smelled her hair sizzle in the flames. Then she felt nothing at all.

He heard the dog whimper and reached his hand out for it, only to have it come away wet. Then he was being shaken, and the pain was almost too much to bear.

"Stop." He cursed in French. When he opened his eyes, it took a moment for his eyes to focus.

"What the hell?" Joseph knelt next to him. Then he pulled out his radio and called for help. His words were muffled as Adam tried to clear his mind. The dog crawled towards him as blood splattered from a large cut just above its shoulder.

He glanced down and assessed his own damage. He was pretty sure he'd broken a rib or two, but other than some scratches, he looked okay. Then he remembered the building and moved to rush towards it. He started calling for Lilly over and over again as the heat grew.

Joseph was trying to pull him back from the fire, but he

needed to get in there, to save Lilly. Even the dog was trying to stop him from rushing towards her.

He collapsed to his knees when reality set in. No one could have survived that! His mind went numb. He'd lost her. The moment he'd waited for all his life had just been ripped out from under him. Happiness was gone. Forever.

Then the dog's head jerked up and he whimpered. When he started crawling towards the tree line, Adam glanced around, hoping. Praying.

"Lilly!" he called out. He listened, watching the dog's ears perk up in reply.

The dog tried to crawl towards the sound he couldn't hear. Adam rushed towards the trees with Joseph on his heels and the dog crawling along.

He must have gone about a fifty feet when he finally heard the soft sound himself.

"Adam," Lilly croaked out.

"Here," he called searching the darkness for her.

Joseph appeared and handed him a flashlight. When he turned it on, he gasped. There, near the foot of a tree was Lilly, her body covered in cuts, blood flowing from almost every exposed spot of skin. Her face was pale white, and her hair was matted around her, singed around the edges.

"Tell me I don't have bangs," she replied, moaning. "I hate bangs." She looked up at him, her blue eyes clouded with pain. "I knew you'd come for me," she whispered when he knelt next to her.

"Don't move her," Joseph called out. "Help's on the way." He turned away and yelled into the radio. "We need a chopper, ASAP!"

Adam felt his heart skip. "I'm here." He brushed a strand of burned hair away from her eyes. "Don't move."

"Okay." She smiled. "For you, I'd do anything," she said, her eyes closing slowly.

"Keep her awake," Joseph called to him.

"Lilly," he said softly, as the dog crouched up next to her body and whimpered. "I know this isn't the right time, but can we have a dog?"

He heard her chuckle and her eyes opened again. "Anything." She smiled. "But I want at least four kids."

"Four?" He smiled down at her, brushing a tear from her dirty face. "I was thinking of five."

"Sounds good." She sighed. "I hurt." She frowned.

"I know, baby. Hang on. I can hear the chopper now." The sound was almost deafening, but he didn't remove his eyes from her face.

"Lilly." He waited until her eyes moved to his. "I'm sorry, baby."

"What?" she asked, her eyes focusing slightly.

"It looks like you've got bangs." He smiled as a tear slipped down his nose and landed softly on her lips.

She licked her lips and smiled. "Salty. Don't cry," she said. "They will grow out."

He laughed and then was pushed away from her as the paramedics took over.

He stood back and watched them shove tubes into her arms, tie her body up tight into a gurney, and load her into a chopper. He held onto the dog until the sound of the blades disappeared. Then he was pushed onto a gurney himself. When they tried to take the dog away, he refused to let go until they promised they would patch him up and keep him until he could pick him up.

As they drove him away, he saw the last embers of the building that had been her prison. He wasn't sure what had happened to Carl, but somehow, he knew the man was no more.

He felt torn. He wanted to hurt the man who had ripped his happiness from him, but at the same time, he was so relieved that Lilly was safe that all his anger was now gone.

All he could think about was Lilly. He couldn't wait to see her again. To hold her in his arms. To kiss her and tell her how much he loved her.

There was no question in his mind that she would be alright. He'd seen it in her eyes as she'd laughed at him. Five kids. They were going to have five kids. He kept saying it over and over again as they worked on him during the drive to the hospital.

"Congrats," one of the paramedics had even said. "I've got three of the little rug rats myself. Number four is in the works right now."

CHAPTER 23

The sounds were the first thing she remembered. French curse words slurring together, so loud that she finally opened her eyes.

"Would you stop cursing," she growled out. When the room turned silent, she smiled. "There, that's much better."

She felt her hands being taken, then kissed.

"I'm sorry, love. I promise never to raise my voice again," Adam said next to her ear.

She snorted, then groaned. "Damn," she said under her breath. "Life would be boring if you kept that promise."

She heard a few chuckles and glanced around, blinking a few times until she could focus.

"Tell me." She took a shallow breath. "How bad are the bangs?"

Several more chuckles echoed in the room. Then Sarah walked over and leaned over her.

"You only have half bangs." She smiled down at her. Lilly could tell she'd been crying. "And half mullet." She ran a hand over her hair. "Sorry, but this whole side of your hair got singed."

"Okay." She rested her face in her sister's hand. "What else?" She looked to Sarah.

When Adam started talking, she shushed him. "You'll tell me what you want me to know, my sister will tell me everything."

Adam frowned down at her. "Go pout somewhere else." She smiled up at him. "Now, talk."

"Well." Sarah looked to Adam, then nodded. "You've got three broken ribs."

"Two more than me," Adam added in.

"You've got burns on the left side. They aren't bad, but you'll be covered in bandages for a while. The doctor doesn't think there will be too much scarring."

"What else?" She could already feel most of it but knew there was something else.

"Um, a broken leg."

"And?" She waited.

"More cuts and bruises than I can count."

"Sarah." She twisted her head around until she could see her friend. "What else?"

She bit her lip. "You were missing part of a finger. But they sewed it back on. They aren't sure if… if it will stay." Her friend's eyes turned red and she started crying.

"Yeah, I figured that." She closed her eyes. "I had to cut the ropes off my legs." She sighed. "Tell me I didn't lose my ring." She wished she could feel the numb digits.

"It's here." A woman with a very thick French accent and long dark hair stepped forward. She held up the ring and smiled. "I'll hold onto it until you're able to fit it back on your finger."

"Lilly, my mother, Adeline." Adam smiled over at the woman and Lilly could see the love in his eyes.

"Okay." She smiled. "Thanks." She turned back to Adam. "Anything else?"

He smiled. "You may have almost lost a knuckle, but you gained a dog named Roscoe." He smiled. "Do you remember him? He was there, he led us to you."

She shook her head. "No, but I love him already then." Everyone laughed. "What about you?" She reached up with her good hand and brushed it down his face.

"Broken rib." He smiled, then frowned. "Cuts and bruises, nothing more." Someone coughed. "Okay." He rolled his eyes. I might have sprained my ankle."

She looked down and saw the crutch under his armpit.

"Why are you standing?" she asked. "Go, sit."

Everyone laughed again. "Why don't we leave these two to talk. Now that we know she's alive." Sarah turned to the room. "Oh, and don't think that getting yourself blown up gets you out of being my new manager," she warned with a smile.

"Never." Lily smiled in return.

After everyone left the room, Adam scooted the chair closer, so he could sit right next to her bed.

"So, what are we going to name them?" he asked.

"What?" She blinked and then decided to just keep her eyes closed.

"The five kids were having."

"Five?" She smiled slightly. "I only remember saying four."

"Yes, but you agreed to five." She felt his fingers brush the side of her neck.

"I was under duress." She could feel the medicine kick in again as the warmth spread up her arm through her IV.

"Yes, but I have years to persuade you to change your mind," he murmured next to her.

When she woke again, the room was dark and she could feel Adam's hand in hers. She heard him breathing lightly and instantly relaxed and slipped back into the darkness.

By the end of the fourth day stuck in the hospital, she was ready to pull out the rest of her singed hair. Her back and butt hurt from laying in the bed so much and she'd been caught trying to use Adam's crutch so much that he'd taken to storing it outside in the hallway when he came in.

"Please," she begged. "Check me out. Take me home. I can't stand one more night in here."

He rolled his eyes. "One more. That's it. Then tomorrow you start physical therapy."

"How about you take me home tonight and we come back for therapy tomorrow?" she pleaded.

"Tomorrow," he promised. Then Sarah and Ben arrived with a stack of DVD's and they all sat around and watched *Bill and Ted's Excellent Adventure*.

Before they left, Rowan walked in, all dressed up, with a pretty brunette following behind him.

"Oh!" she exclaimed. "The party." She'd totally forgotten that she'd promised to go with Rowan to his party.

"It's okay." He smiled. "You had an excuse." He leaned down and placed a soft kiss on her cheek. "Besides, I hear you're already taken." He shook Adam's hand. "This is Kayla Thomas…"

"His date for the night." She stepped forward and

smiled down at him. "We're old school friends. Actually, Rowan used to date my sister Lori," she added.

"Yes," Lilly remembered. "I've heard of you, well, your sister, before." Lilly glanced over at Sarah, who was frowning into her lap. "Are you back in town? I heard you were…"

"In New York for school. Yes, I've moved back and ran into Rowan the other day, and since you were tied up." She smiled. "He invited me to fill in for you. I heard you had quite the adventure."

She chuckled. "I guess you could say that."

"I also hear that congratulations are in order." She nodded to Adam. Then, in fluent French, she said, "Congratulations, may your life together be as adventurous and as powerful as your coming together."

Adam smiled, then looked over to Rowan and winked. "I like this one."

Rowan coughed and turned a little red. "Well, we should be going. We don't want to be late." He took Kayla's hand and practically dragged her from the room.

"What was that all about?" Lilly turned to Sarah who just rolled her eyes.

"Let's just pray that she didn't turn out anything like her sister," she added.

"Didn't her sister die when she was—"

"Sixteen. Yes, on the night of Rowan's sixteenth birthday party. Right after he'd broken up with her."

"That's right," Lilly added.

"I sure hope he knows what he's getting himself into." Sarah frowned at the closed door. "I don't think he could stand to go through something like that again."

"What? Loss?" Adam asked.

"No, dealing with a bitch who cheated and manipulated him, then caused her own death because she was a psycho." Sarah turned to Lilly and gasped. "I'm sorry."

"What?" She blinked. "Why?"

"Carl." The name was a whisper in the room.

"It's okay." She smiled. "For all of Carl's faults, with his last breath, he tried to save me." She smiled and reached for Adam's hand. She'd told him everything that had happened and had relayed it to the police for their reports. "In his twisted way, he just wanted to keep me safe." She shook her head and felt her skin shiver. "Okay, enough of that..." She broke off when the door opened again. Expecting a nurse, she smiled at the woman who entered. Then she felt every ounce of blood drain from her face as she stared back at her own eyes. Only these were older, sadder, and empty of almost any love.

"Mother?" It came out as a whisper.

Adam sat in the corner and watched Lilly closely. He refused to leave the room even when she had told him she would be fine. Everyone else had vacated quickly, but not Adam.

His eyes had raked over the woman. Scanning for... well, he didn't know what. Emotion? All he knew was that he wasn't going to leave Lilly to deal with all the emotions alone. He'd made himself a promise that he would never leave her alone to deal with anything again. Especially her past.

"I understand your hesitation in agreeing to see me. When I heard what had happened..." Carolina glanced in his direction and twisted her hands together, a move he'd seen Lilly do herself on multiple occasions. "Well, I was worried and figured…" Her tone was flat.

"Thank you for the flowers." She nodded towards the bouquet of pink carnations, which sat among a wall of brightly colored flowers and balloons from everyone else. "And thank you for making the trip from Atlanta."

"Oh." She nodded. "I read what happened to you. I'm sorry you had to go through something like that." There was no emotion in her voice and Adam was beginning to wonder if the woman had any at all.

Lilly's eyebrows shot up. "Something like…" She chuckled, and Adam could see the hurt. "You mean, sorry I had to be blown up? Is that what it takes for you to feel remorse?"

"I…" Her mother shook her head, then he watched her chin rise. "I know you're angry with me about the past, but I'm a changed woman. I had to hold down three jobs just to keep food in your mouth."

"Is that how you justified it?" She shifted. "You told yourself you were too busy to deal with the problems? Or did you even have a problem with what Dave did to me? Maybe you got off knowing what he was doing?" She shifted when Adam's hand reached out to touch her, to calm her. She jerked her hand away. "No, I understand that you've made nice with your mother, but your mother didn't idly sit by while her husband fucked her teenage daughter every night." She was almost screaming it.

"You watch your tone with me," Carolina warned.

"Or what?" Lilly sat forward. "Let's get one thing straight. I forgive you. I forgive you and the moment you walk out that door, I will forget you. You have no place in my new life, nor in the life, I will build with my own family. I replaced you, years ago, with a woman who would fight to the gates of hell to make sure I was happy and safe. I have a sister who, even there's no blood between us, would gladly give up everything she has to do the same." She glanced over at Adam and a tear slipped down her cheek. "I have a man who would do everything in his power to see me smile, even with his or my dying breath." Her eyes turned slowly back towards her mother. "So, go. Live your changed life and know that I am well, despite anything you've ever done."

Carolina looked between him and Lilly, then without a word and without shedding a tear, turned and walked out of the room.

Adam got up, picked up the pink flowers, walked them to the trash, and dumped them in. Then he walked over and wrapped his arms around Lilly and held her as she cried.

"Well played, my love," he murmured into her hair.

Less than a minute later, Sarah and Crystal rushed in. "Is that bitch still here?" Crystal said, glancing around.

"I called mom." Sarah smiled and walked over to wrap her arms around Lilly. "I figured you would need us."

Lilly sniffled and nodded. "I do." She held on as her family wrapped their arms around each other. Crystal held out an arm to him and he joined in.

"There, now the universe is righted." Crystal nodded as a tear slid down her face. "Don't you fret anymore about your past. I read your chart this morning and I see only happiness from here on out." She glanced towards Adam and winked. "And there are five rings around your universe." She turned to Lilly.

"Mother," Sarah warned. "You can't possibly…"

"Shush." She waved towards Sarah. "Serenity Sunshine Holley, I've told you to leave reading charts to me."

Ben coughed from the corner. "I think you mean, Serenity Sunshine Rothschild." He smiled and walked over to wrap his arm around his wife.

"Yes," Crystal smiled. "Of course, I do." She tilted her head and wiggled her eyebrows. "I read your chart this morning too."

Sarah groaned and rolled her eyes.

"What did it say?" Ben asked.

"Don't, you're only egging her on," Sarah croaked.

Lilly laughed. "I would like to hear too."

"Let's just say, twins run in our family." Crystal laughed when Sarah slapped playfully at her as she rushed around the room, giggling.

Adam couldn't help but laugh and realize that he had the best family in the world. A family that stuck together no matter what and one that knew how to laugh and, more importantly, one that knew how to love.

This is a work of fiction. Names, characters, places, and incidents are either the product of the author's imagination or are used fictitiously, and any resemblance to actual persons, living or dead, business establishments, events, or locales is entirely coincidental.

FRENCH KISS

PRINT ISBN: 978-1-942896-70-8

DIGITAL ISBN: 978-1-942896-69-2

Copyeditor: Erica Ellis – inkdeepediting.com

Missy's Moment

Breaking Travis

Roping Ryan

Wild Bride

Corey's Catch

Tessa's Turn

The Grayton Series

Last Resort

Someday Beach

Rip Current

In Too Deep

Swept Away

High Tide

Lucky Series

Unlucky In Love

Sweet Resolve

Best of Luck

A Little Luck

Silver Cove Series

Silver Lining

French Kiss

Happy Accident

Hidden Charm

A Silver Cove Christmas

Entangled Series – Paranormal Romance

The Awakening

The Beckoning

The Ascension

Haven, Montana Series

Closer to You

Never Let Go

Holding On

Pride Oregon Series

A Dash of Love

My Kind of Love

Season of Love

Tis the Season

Dare to Love

Where I Belong

Wildflowers Series

Summer Nights

Summer Heat

Stand Alone Books

Twisted Rock

For a complete list of books:

http://JillSanders.com

ABOUT THE AUTHOR

Jill Sanders is a New York Times, USA Today, and international bestselling author of Sweet Contemporary Romance, Romantic Suspense, Western Romance, and Paranormal Romance novels. With over 55 books in eleven series, translations into several different languages, and audiobooks there's plenty to choose from. Look for Jill's bestselling stories wherever romance books are sold or visit her at jillsanders.com

Jill comes from a large family with six siblings, including an identical twin. She was raised in the Pacific Northwest and later relocated to Colorado for college and a successful IT career before discovering her talent for writing sweet and sexy page-turners. After Colorado, she decided to move south, living in Texas and now making her home along the Emerald Coast of Florida. You will find that the settings of several of her series are inspired by her time spent living in these areas. She has two sons and off-set the testosterone in her house by adopting three furry little ladies that provide her company while she's locked in her writing cave. She enjoys heading to the beach, hiking, swimming, wine-tasting, and pickleball with her husband, and of course writing. If you have read any of her books, you may also notice that there is a love of food, especially sweets! She has been blamed for a few added pounds by her assistant, editor, and fans... donuts or pie anyone?

facebook.com/JillSandersBooks

twitter.com/JillMSanders

bookbub.com/authors/jill-sanders

www.ingramcontent.com/pod-product-compliance
Lightning Source LLC
Chambersburg PA
CBHW071237190726

48292CB00007B/2333